Lock Down Publications and Ca$h
Presents

SUPER GREMLIN 4

The First Slimeto

By
KING RIO

Stay Connected with Us!

Text **LOCKDOWN** to 22828 to stay up-to-date with new releases, sneak peaks, contests and more…

Like our page on Facebook:
Lock Down Publications

Join Lock Down Publications/The New Era Reading Group

Visit our website:
www.lockdownpublications.com

Follow us on Instagram:
Lock Down Publications

Email Us: We want to hear from you!

Prologue

One of them snatched the black pillowcases off Whitney Clarrett's head, and she looked up at them, the three men who'd kidnapped her from the parking lot outside of Redbone's Gentleman's Club.

All three of them wore ski masks. Each mask was a different color — red, gray, and black. The tall, slender man in the gray mask stood in front of the other two, a Glock with an extended clip tightly gripped in one gloved hand, the black pillowcase dangling loosely from the fingertips of his other gloved hand. She could only tell they were Black men from the skin around their eyes and mouths; they wore long sleeved, designer sweatshirts, black, leather gloves, and high-end designer jeans, thoroughly preventing her from seeing other portions of their skin.

"Look, bitch," said Gray Mask. "I'm going to take that tape off your mouth, and when I do, you better start talkin'. You gon tell me where your man took all that dope. You do that, and you'll make it back to your kids in one piece. You don't do that; I don't know how many pieces you'll end up in. We clear on that?"

Whitney nodded her head vehemently. She'd suspected the kidnapping had something to do with the robbery of Markio's stash house. After all, it had been her idea to send her boyfriend, Voltaire, and his Haitian gang to rob the rural northwest Indiana home. She'd spoken with Voltaire immediately after the robbery. "We got a few hundred bricks," he'd said over the FaceTime call. "Looks like dog food, fentanyl. and coke. Millions of dollars' worth of products. If all this dope is as pure as it smells, I'll be able to at least give you a million and half in the next couple of weeks."

The news had brightened Whitney's spirits, made her feel like she'd finally won the battle against Markio Earl, that bastard ex-boyfriend of hers who'd fucked her out of 2.5 million in cash last summer.

Now, her spirits weren't feeling all the business. She'd pissed herself a couple of hours ago, and her orange, sequined Dior dress was still wet around the ass. One of the men had taken her fifty-thousand-dollar, white diamond, Cuban link necklace while another removed the icy Cartier watch from her wrist. Her orange, leather, Hermes Birkin bag, for which Voltaire had paid the exorbitant price of $87,999.98 plus taxes and shipping fees, was also gone, as well as the thousand-dollar packet of bank new hundreds she'd had inside of it.

Not that she cared about any of those material things. She just wanted to make it out of this godforsaken westside of Chicago basement with her heart beating and her brain in working order. Though she had to admit that her material blessings did indeed factor into her will to survive. She had $1,352,732.09 in her Bank of America business account and an additional $425,830.48 in her personal checking account, more than enough to make up for the material losses. Her cosmetics company — iKiss Kosmetics — was worth $3.8 million and had a brand new iKiss store she'd opened in Miami just yesterday. For the past six months, she'd been living with Voltaire at Star Island, a thirty-million-dollar mansion in Miami Beach, Florida. Her four teenage children resided in Michigan City, Indiana, her hometown, but they lived in a house she owned in its entirely, and none of them wanted for a thing. She'd made it out the hood and was soaring above the poverty line, but her success meant nothing if she wasn't alive to enjoy it with her family.

Gray Mask ripped the duct tape from her lips. She winced and started breathing through her open mouth. Hyperventilating really. Her pretty, yellowish brown face was sweaty and tear streaked. The pillowcase over her head for so many hours had broken her. She was ready to tell them whatever they wanted to know.

Raising his Glock and pressing the barrel against her forehead, Gray Mask said, "Bitch, if you even try to scream…"

"I won't. I promise," Whitney said shakily. Her gaze fluctuated between the trio of armed men, studying the eye holes in their masks. "Voltaire and his boys got an Airbnb somewhere in Roseland. It's on the southside of Chicago. I believe on 119th and LaSalle. That's all I know. If you let me see my phone, I can text him and get the exact address."

Red Mask chuckled and moved forward a step. He was tall and chubby, sneering at her as he smoked a Newport cigarette. The butt end of a black pistol and its extended magazine was sticking out from the front right-hand pocket of his jeans. "You must think we slow or some'n," he said. He tapped a pull of ash onto Whitney's face. "The fuck we look like letting you use your phone?"

"I swear on my kids it's the truth," she said. "That's where they took that box truck. He said three of his boys got killed during the robbery, but they made it out with a bunch of kilos. Bricks of heroin and cocaine and fentanyl. I swear to God."

Red Mask turned to look at Gray Mask. Whitney got the sense that Gray Mask was the alpha male of this three man show. His body language was aggressive and dominant, his dark eyes cold and calculating. She eyed the diamond bezel of a Rolex Sky Dweller on his right wrist. It further cemented her suspicion that he and his crew were upper echelon gang members, the kind that usually entrusted lower-ranking foot soldiers with handling their dirty work. Someone had to have offered them a large sum of money to make such a risky move themselves. Kidnapping her from the crowded parking lot of a popular strip club could have gone wrong in a hundred ways. That sort of risk was worth six figures at the very least.

This brazen kidnapping had "Millionaire Markio" written all over it.

"Grab a few of the bros," Gray Mask said to his red masked partner in crime. He tucked his Glock pistol behind his black, leather, Louis Vuitton belt. "I want y'all to drive out there and post up on 119th and LaSalle. I think Gooly and Tone Bone still run it for the CVLs over there. Tell 'em I sent y'all and ask 'em if they know of any Airbnb rentals on that block." He turned to Whitney and asked, "What kind of car they drive?"

"A black Escalade and a black Chevy Trailblazer," she said, the words spilling out of her in a single breath.

Gray Mask nodded his head, and Red Mask walked off and disappeared into the basement stairwell, puffing his cigarette as he went. A few seconds later, Whitney heard the metallic thump of the bulkhead door slamming shut. She looked behind Gray Mask and saw that his black masked comrade — a man who was a few inches shorter and perhaps a hundred pounds heavier than Red Mask — was stroking the growing bulge in the front of his jeans, jeans that fit him snugly enough to show the entire outline of his hardening penis. The shimmering puddle of urine beneath Whitney's chair made her feel disgusting, but it didn't seem to bother Black Mask at all. He moved forward, took hold of the strip of duct tape that still clung to one side of her mouth, and pressed it firmly over her lips as Gray Mask took out a smartphone and left the room.

"I don't trust that hole," Black Mask muttered. He picked up a boxcutter from a nearby table and used the sharp blade to cut through the duct tape that bound her ankles to the chair, kneeling in front of her and peeking up her dress as he did it. "Ain't nothing wrong with the other ones though. Pussy ain't got no teeth."

"At least let me shower first," was what Whitney tried to say. With the duct tape on her mouth, it came out, "Mm mm mm," and she immediately realized how incoherent it sounded. Her hands were taped together behind the chair. She struggled to free them as Black Mask pushed her dress up around her waist and rubbed his gloved fingertips between her vaginal lips. He inserted one finger and slid it in and out for a couple of seconds. Then, he added a second finger and a third. She tried squeezing her legs shut and received a hard punch to the chin for her efforts.

"You got to be one of the baddest bitches I ever met in my life," Black Mask whispered as he continued to penetrate her with his three fat fingers. "On my son, if it wasn't for this whole situation, I would've gave you five racks for some of this pussy. But seein' as you done fucked over my homie, I guess that makes this free, huh?"

Whitney closed her eyes and cringed, feeling the coolness of her tears as they began to trickle down her cheeks. She gagged and swallowed the bile that rose up into her throat. In all her thirty-six years of living, she'd never came close to experiencing a rape. She felt hopeless. Powerless. Defenseless.

Seconds later, as she opened her eyes and watched the morbidly obese man in the black ski mask tug an extra-large Magnum condom out of the front, left hand pocket of his dark blue jeans, she looked past him, hoping to find Gray Mask walking toward her, returning to save her from this rapidly unfolding sexual assault.

But Gray Mask was nowhere in sight. He'd stepped into a utility closet and shut the door behind him. She could hear him talking on the phone, but the sound of the voice was too muffled for her to comprehend what he was saying.

Black Mask undid his belt and dropped his jeans and boxer briefs to his ankles, and Whitney drew in a deep breath that flared her nostrils and inflated her lungs to capacity.

The fat man's dick was huge — at least twelve inches in length and thick too — a long, black, veiny muscle sticking straight out in front of him. He enclosed one hand around his fat erection and stroked it roughly as he kicked out of his jeans and underwear and used his teeth to tear open the golden condom wrapper.

Whitney shut her eyes as he lifted her legs onto his shoulders. She thought, *Oh, my God, this man is about to split me in two!* She felt his cockhead rubbing up and down her vaginal lips, and she held her breath as he eased it into her tight little hole.

Her eyes popped open as he went in deeper, his mammoth erection stretching her vaginal walls to the limit. She gasped. She'd had some big dicks before, but this was something else entirely. Whoever was behind that black mask had a dick that defied all knowledge of human anatomy. He wasted no time in establishing a pounding rhythm, knocking all the breath out of her as he did it. All Whitney could do was look up at him with gasping eyes, moaning deep in her throat and creaming all over his length as he fucked her.

A minute or two in, he lifted her aching chin and planted a kiss on the gray duct tape that covered her mouth. It was a violent kiss, the opposite of compassionate, and it sent her body into convulsions as she trembled her way through the most powerful orgasm she'd experienced all year.

"You wet pussy havin ass bitch," he said, leaning into his thrusts and pushing her legs way up in the air. The wooden chair creaked noisily and steadily. And then, the two rear legs snapped like toothpicks, and he came crashing down on top of her, the weight of his corpulent body driving his oversized erection deep in her stomach as they landed hard on the smooth concrete floor.

Whitney's eyes bulged out of their sockets. A part of her hated what the stranger was doing to her, but there was also a part of her that didn't want him to stop. He went on fucking her as if the chair hadn't just broken to pieces beneath them. Beyond his shoulder, Whitney saw Gray Mask step out of the utility closet with his head kind of tilted to the side as he took in the scene ten feet ahead of him. He pocketed his smartphone, folded his arms across his chest, and stood there, staring at them for a long, silent moment.

Then, a subtle smirk formed in the mouth hole of his gray ski mask, and as the fat man continued to fuck Whitney senseless, she watched a familiar looking bulge grow in the front of Gray Mask's black, Amiri jeans.

It was at that moment that Whitney began to have mixed feelings about this whole kidnapping ordeal. On the one hand, she wanted to get away from these masked criminals as soon as possible. But on the other hand, if their method of torture was going to be fucking the life out of her the way the fat man was doing her now — he currently had his face buried in the crook of her neck and her legs pushed way up to near her head, breathing hot, alcohol-scented breaths against her ear as he slammed his dick in and out of her — she thought she might not mind staying here a little while longer.

Chapter 1

At 6:51 in the morning, 119th and LaSalle was a cold, quiet street with only the gentle whistle of the wind and the occasional rumble of a passing motorist disturbing the peace. A parking authority van idled on the street toward one end of the block. Ten feet behind, a young, Black woman stood guard next to a silver-colored Toyota Tacoma while her partner, a middle-aged Black man with graying facial hair, squatted low on his haunches to attach a boot to the front driver's side tire.

The truck parked directly ahead of the Tacoma was a black Cadillac Escalade. A black Chevy Trailblazer had just pulled in two car lengths ahead of the Escalade. A single Black man with long, fat dreadlocks exited the driver's door of the Trailblazer carrying two large McDonald's bags and a tray of beverages. He was heavyset and dark in complexion, wearing a black, leather, bomber jacket over sweatpants and Nike sneakers.

"You want me to hop out and whack this nigga?"

Markio voiced no answer to the question. He simply shook his head and watched as the man crossed the street and ascended the concrete porch steps of a redbrick, two-story home. He knocked twice on the door, stomped the snow from his shoes, and then entered without waiting for someone to open the door for him.

"That's the house right there," Markio said to Lil Luke, the coldhearted, young shooter he was looking at on his iPhone screen. "Run in that bitch and lay everybody down. If a nigga reaches for any kind of weapon — shit, y'all know what to do."

He ended the FaceTime call and sat silently in the luxurious comfort of his girlfriend, Nikkia's black Mercedes Benz Sprinter van, puffing on a thick blunt of exotic marijuana while seven members of his gang spilled out of the two blacked out Hellcats parked ahead of him — a Dodge Charger and a Dodge Challenger. All seven of the young men were Traveling Vice Lords, and since they all honored and adhered to the strict laws of the Almighty Vice Lord Nation, they followed every order Markio gave them.

Just last night, while seated at a VIP table inside of Redbone's Gentleman's Club with several of the gang's highest-ranking members, Markio had been given the rank of 3-star Universal Elite, which gave him limited authority over several hundred lower ranking and non-ranking members of the gang.

And he knew exactly how to utilize that authority.

Markio's number one rule was to never ask a fellow gang member to do something he wouldn't do himself. The mission he was sending them on now was risky, but this situation called for drastic measures. Yesterday evening, he'd had over a hundred kilos of cocaine, twenty kilos of heroin, and twenty-eight kilos of fentanyl taken from his northwest Indiana stash house in a robbery that left his nephew, Tyquan, and close friend, Fat Jerm, wounded and three of the robbers dead. When police responded to the report of shots fired, they'd found not only the three dead but also Markio's last twelve bricks of fentanyl and well over two thousand pounds of Black Cherry Gelato marijuana, which went for $6,000 a pound. He'd taken a major loss at the hands of Voltaire and his Haitian gang, and one way or another, someone was going to pay for it.

Sitting in the soft, white leather seat, wearing a black Louis Vuitton jogger and matching LV sneakers with

$450,000 worth of diamond jewelry encircling his neck and wrists, Markio looked exactly like the ghetto millionaire he'd become six months ago when he and his then girlfriend, Whitney Clarrett, had gone to a storage auction in search of furniture.

Markio had purchased a locker for its living room and bedroom sets, and it was only later that he'd discovered more than $5 million in cash stuffed inside the eight stainless steel suitcases he'd gotten out of the locker. In the months since, thanks to his connections within Mexico's infamous Matamoros Cartel, he'd been able to turn that $5 million into $14 million.

But if he didn't get those stolen drugs back, he'd have to pay the $9.4 million he owed the cartel out of his own pockets. It was this possibility that had him on edge.

The man seated across from Markio had a red ski mask pushed up on his forehead. He was called Apple by all who knew him, and he'd lost a considerable amount of weight in the years since he was found shot up next to a west side restaurant a few years back. He'd gone to grab a few Italian beef sandwiches during war times and had paid the price. He and Markio went way back. Markio had known Apple ever since they were kids in the early nineties when they'd spent all their days and nights on Trumbull Avenue. Apple was still a little overweight, but he was nowhere near as heavy as he'd been before he was shot.

"I think Chubb and Rev gon fuck around and rape your girl," he said matter of factly as he reached for Markio's blunt. "That nigga, Chubb, was staring hard as hell at the thick ass bitch before I left them in that basement. You know they tried to rape Mary's sister a couple weeks ago."

"That ain't my bitch," Markio said with a shrug. He took another drag on the blunt and ignored Apple's outstretched hand. His red-veined eyes were focused on the house his seven young bulls were approaching. "I don't think they'll rape her though. We grew up with them niggas. They ain't no fucking rapists."

"Man, fuck them. Pass the weed, old petty ass nigga," Apple said, leaning halfway out of his seat now.

Markio chuckled twice and kept on smoking, gazing fixedly out the Sprinter van's darkly tinted side window as his gang rushed in through the front door of the house where he suspected his drugs were being stored.

The parking authority woman didn't even glance at the group of young Black men as they barged into the house. Markio drew in another mouthful of potent marijuana smoke and then moved forward to the edge of his seat, passing the blunt to Apple as he did it. Apple rudely snatched the blunt from his hand, eliciting another chuckle from Markio, who turned and looked at his old friend with a glint of amusement in his squinted red eyes.

Markio was about to mutter a snide remark when the iPhone on his lap rang again. It was another FaceTime call from Lil Luke, a grimy young nigga from Markio's neighborhood who had just beaten a double murder conviction on appeal not even a year ago. He'd killed some chick named Chandra and a nigga named Marshall on the doorstep of some exotic dancer's apartment, and the dancer ended up snitching on him. The stripper, a badass young redbone named Tamia, later recanted her statement and testified on Lil Luke's behalf, claiming that two crooked CPD homicide detectives had coerced her into fingering him as the killer.

When the FaceTime call began, Lil Luke had a stunned look on his face. "You ain't gon' believe this shit, big homie," he said, switching to the rear facing camera. "Look at these niggas. They over with."

He panned the camera across the dining room, and Markio's brow rose in shock as he viewed the two purple faced men who were seated around the table in tall backed wooden chairs. There was an open kilo of what Markio knew

14

was pure fentanyl on the table near the man who was slumped back in his chair. A rolled up fifty-dollar bill lay next to a thin line of white powder in front of him. The second man had his head resting on his folded arms, his eyes wide and lifeless, a worm of white foam suspended from one corner of his mouth. They were two of the men Markio had seen on the Ring home security footage of the stash house robbery.

"Don't touch nothin," Markio said quickly. "They overdosed. That's pure fentanyl on that table. Look for Keondre Muck's brother. He should be there too."

"We can just ask him." Lil Luke turned the camera toward the living room where three members of the gang were ordering the driver of the Trailblazer to strip.

The man looked terrified, and he had good reason to be. There were two Glocks with extended clips pointed at his head as he removed his jacket with trembling hands and tossed it onto the arm of the easy chair behind him. He was also one of the men that Markio had witnessed robbing his stash house.

"Where Voltaire at?" Markio asked through the phone.

The man looked at the back of Lil Luke's phone with apprehension wrinkling his forehead. "I don't know. He was here when I left," the man said, shaking.

Lil Luke swung a gun at his face, striking him just outside of his right eye and opening a deep laceration that immediately began to spout out blood. The man stumbled back a few feet, bringing one hand up to the fresh gash in his face just as a phone started ringing from somewhere inside the room. The man looked down at his pants pocket, and Lil Luke reached inside it to retrieve the phone. He held it up in front of the camera, and Markio saw the name Voltaire along with a contact photo that depicted Voltaire leaning back against the chrome grills of a black Rolls Royce sedan with Whitney leaning back against him, his strong, dark arms wrapped tight around her waist, a warm smile on her gorgeous, yellowish face, an unreadable expression on his.

"Answer it," Markio said coldly.

Lil Luke answered the call and put it on speaker before holding it up to the bleeding man's mouth. When he hesitated to speak, Big Keanan, a twenty-seven-year-old TVL, who was just as fleshy around the middle as Apple, jammed the barrel of his Glock against the man's jaw.

"Yeah," the man said. Blood trickled down from between his fingers as he held the side of his face. Tears fell from his frightened eyes and rolled down over his cheeks before coming together beneath his trembling chin and dripping down onto the belly of his brown Adidas sweatshirt.

"Listen to me, Woppo. Do not go back to the Airbnb," Voltaire said, panicky. "Ronnie and Milk... Man.... they... they snorted some dope after we loaded those boxes back into the box truck. I think it was fentanyl. I sat in the bedroom after you left, talking to Whitney's daughter, Eva, and when I came out, I found them dead at the dining room table. There was nothing I could do. I had to get out of there."

"I see that. I just walked in," Woppo told him.

"Get out of there asap. Find yourself a hotel room and wait for my call. I'm heading to Whitney's old place in Indiana. I still haven't heard from her, but her kids are there. I'm gonna stay with them until we find out who took her and whether or not it has anything to do with the bricks we took from the ex-boy. We may have to drive this box truck all the way back to the three oh five because there's no way we can ship this much product through the mail."

"Okay. Let me get outta here. I'll call you," Woppo said and nodded for Lil Luke to end the call.

Lil Luke ended the call, and before Markio could say anything, Big Keanan fired a single shot through the side of Woppo's head. The big man dropped like a sack of cinderblocks. Markio looked up from his phone and saw the parking authority woman's head swing around to look for the source of the gunshot. Markio's sister, Shakia, who'd been his personal driver for the past several months, started the engine and quickly pulled off from the curb.

Markio wanted to ask Big Keanan what the fuck he was thinking, but Lil Luke ended the video call, and Apple passed Markio the blunt. Shakia lowered the black glass partition that separated the driver's cabin from the rear passengers' cabin and shouted, "Man, fuck that, bruh. We outta here." So, all Markio could do was sit back and fill his lungs with exotic weed smoke, listening to the Est Gee song that had begun to boom from the speakers as the Sprinter rocketed forward.

He got a text from Lil Luke a few minutes later. "Jaybo grabbed that brick off the table. What you want us to do with it?"

"Give it to Big K." Markio wrote back. Big Keanan had just murdered a man for Markio, and he felt the kilo of fentanyl — minus the gram or two that had killed Ronnie and Milk-Man — was well worth the body.

If Big Keanan wouldn't have jumped the gun, Markio would have had the gang hold Woppo hostage until he got his bricks back. But Woppo was dead now, and he didn't really need anything more from Woppo anyway. Voltaire was going to Whitney's old place, and Markio knew exactly where that old place was located — 302 East Comb Street, Michigan City, Indiana. He would make a quick stop at the South Shore train station downtown to pick up his cousin, Jarvon, who'd flown in from Baton Rouge sometime last night, and then, he'd be on his way with Lil Luke and the rest of the gang not far behind him.

At least those were his plans.

Chapter 2

Wearing only a plain gray pair of sweatpants and dirty-bottomed, white ankle socks, forty-nine-year-old Steven Grenshaw sat on his sister Kanitra's raggedy, old, shit-colored sofa and watched the morning news.

A kidnapping had taken place on the parking lot of a strip club just a few blocks southeast of Kanitra's three-bedroom apartment, which took up the first floor of a ramshackle three flat near the corner of 13th and Sawyer. The kidnapping victim's name was Whitney Clarrett, and she looked exactly like the kind of woman Steven "Steel" Grenshaw had seen in all the urban culture magazines during his twenty-year stint in the Illinois prison system, the kind of woman you might see dancing in a Megan Thee Stallion video or on the arm of some famous athlete. She was a yellow bone with a perfect face, a waterfall of straight, black hair, and a mouthwateringly curvaceous body. A brief video of her crying children — three teenage girls who looked just as beautiful as their missing mother — revealed that she was the owner of a successful cosmetics company.

"Ay, Neetra! You heard of this Whitney bitch? The bitch who got kidnapped last night?" Steel yelled as he leaned forward to grab his cigarettes off the chipped and scarred wooden coffee table in front of him.

A notably loud creak resonated from the floorboards in Neetra's bedroom as she climbed down from her bed, and then she appeared in her doorway, dressed in the five

18

hundred dollar pink Fendi robe Steel had bought for her when she took him shopping on his first day home from prison. She was tall and thick, ten years younger than Steel, and just as unattractive in the face as their mother. She and Steel had different fathers, and because Steel's father, a retired computer engineer, had died three years ago, leaving him a six-figure fortune, Kanitra hadn't hesitated to hold her brother down until the parole board granted him his freedom. He'd been sending her money over the three years since he received his inheritance, a few thousand dollars here and there, and it seemed like she'd blown it all on hair, nails, and designer fashion. Her big, round ass was undeniably her most appealing feature, and she kept it on full display, constantly posting mirror selfies to social media in booty shorts, yoga pants, and skintight jeans and dresses, likely to detract from her less than attractive facial features.

"Nah," she said, eyeing her freshly manicured fingernails. "I don't know that hoe. I read in the comments on IG that she used to date Markio a while back. That's all I know so far."

"Markio the author? The nigga who wrote *The Bird Man*?"

"Mm hm. He one of them punk ass Travelers from off 15th and Trumbull. You know I don't fuck with none of them."

Steel's cool expression hardened into a monstrous scowl as he turned back to the television. The news anchor had moved on to another top story — some cop named Richard Westman and three others had been killed in a gang shootout on 15th and Homan a few days ago, and several others had been wounded, but Steel's malevolent thoughts remained on Markio, the writer whose novels he'd seen numerous inmates reading during his last few months at Menard Correctional Center. He'd chosen not to read them himself, not because he didn't enjoy a good urban fiction novel but because the author of the book series was rumored to be associated with the TVLs who'd murdered his son in July of 2016.

Durron "Cash Boy" Grenshaw had been sitting in his car with his close friend, B-Man, parked in front of B-Man's girlfriend, Chandra's house on 16th and Spaulding when someone jumped out of a gray pickup truck and riddled the car with bullets. Forty-eight 7.62-millimeter shell casings were found at the scene, and no one was ever arrested for the crime.

But the streets knew who was responsible. The 15th street TVLs and the black Gangster New Breeds from 13th and Sawyer were warring heavily at the time, and they'd caught two Breeds on their turf. There were rumors that Chandra had set them up, but she was shot and killed later that same summer, so there would be no answers from her.

"I knew Markio was locked up when they killed Durron," Neetra said, "but he's affiliated with the niggas who did it so fuck him too." She plopped down next to her older brother, her attention on her smartphone as she uploaded a photo to Instagram. "And do you know what's crazy? The nigga, Markio, just got a fuckin movie deal with MTN Studios. That's Alexus Costilla's production company. I just watched a video of him signing the contract. One of his sisters posted the video on her TikTok, but it's everywhere now. They ain't said how much money he got, but it has to be at least ten or twenty million. Alexus is worth over two hundred billion now, and the last thing she posted on IG was a picture of her and Markio at the Versace mansion."

"Hm." Steel sucked on his cigarette, lost in thought. He'd only been home from prison three days. He'd spent $30,000 on a brand-new Nissan Rogue and about five grand on clothes and other necessities, and he still had almost three hundred thousand dollars in the bank. He planned on using the money to buy himself a house somewhere in the suburbs and one or two rental properties here in the city.

But all that would have to wait because the first thing on his mind was avenging his son's murder.

Neetra handed him her phone, and he watched a jealousy-inducing video of Markio Earl signing a contract while several richly dressed Black women stood nearby, cheering and applauding. The video only served to exacerbate Steel's anger toward Markio and the set of TVLs he represented. He gave the phone back and smashed his cigarette out in the ashtray.

Steel was just about to rise from the sofa to walk off the anger when Neetra pushed him back and slipped her hand into his sweatpants. The feel of her fingers closing around his dick calmed him down in an instant. She began to stroke his flaccid member inside of his sweats, and soon, it was growing in her hand.

"Chill out, Steel," she said and kissed the ball of his shoulder, right on the spot where her name was tattooed across a fat heart. "You just got out. Give it some time. We'll get them niggas for what they did to our son."

"Nah, fuck that. Fuck waiting. I want you to call Pojo and Skip. Tell 'em I got a few grand for them to go over there on 15th and lay one of them Travelers down today."

"Okay. Just give me a few minutes. Let me get you right first."

Steel settled into his seat as Neetra released his dick from his sweats and went down on him, wrapping her fat lips around the head of his thick, black erection and taking his entire six-inch length into her mouth. She moved her knee up onto the couch, and he rubbed all over her ass while her head went up and down in his lap.

He thought of his deceased son and wondered what his family would think of him if they knew he was Durron's true father. They were under the impression that all six of Neetra's children were a product of her relationship with Sean Newsome, the ex-husband of hers who was now serving a two hundred forty month sentence in federal prison.

The incestuous relationship she and Steel had shared since she was twelve years old was a secret they would take to the grave.

Chapter 3

Each of the two Louis Vuitton duffel bags Markio kept with him at all times contained $250,000 in cash, all of it untaxed proceeds from the hundreds of pounds of his high-grade marijuana he'd sold over the past six months. His Patek Philippe wristwatch was drenched in flawless white diamonds, as were his two Cuban link necklaces and the large "MARKIO" pendant that hung down from one of them. Even before the millions, when he was just a low-level heroin and weed dealer, he'd taken all the necessary steps to keep up his appearance — not only for the women in his life but also for the sake of his paternal family's pristine reputation in the streets of Chicago.

So when he picked up his cousin, Jarvon Barnett, alias J-Slime, from the train stop downtown and saw that Jarvon was wearing scuffed Nike sneakers, an old pair of jeans, and a green *NEVER BROKE AGAIN* hoodie, he reached in one of his duffel bags and handed J-Slime a ten-thousand-dollar, rubber-banded stack of hundreds and then directed Shakia to the Gold Coast shopping district.

J-Slime's face lit up with a smile that showed all sixteen of his sparkling gold teeth. "I will need a stick," he said, eyeing the three guns that were visible inside the open duffel bag.

They were Markio's two .40 caliber Glock model 23 pistols and his mini-Draco assault pistol. Markio reached in and lifted out one of the Glocks — not the one with the fifty

23

round drum magazine but the one with the thirty round extended clip.

"You already got one in the chamber," Markio said, relighting the last three inches of his blunt. "Be careful with that switch. It'll empty that whole clip in two seconds."

"I already know, Slime," said J-Slime, and Markio chuckled at the blood gang terminology. Until now, he'd only heard it in rap songs. J-Slime tucked the pistol and shook hands with Markio, which allowed Markio to see the "38" tattoo on the back of his right hand.

Markio shot a quick glance at the back of J-Slime's other hand and saw that "Chippewa St." was inked there. He was a lanky kid, maybe 6'2", and around twenty-one years of age, brown skinned with short, kinky, black hair and vigilant brown eyes. There were a number of scars on his face and hands. He offered a slight head nod to Apple and then turned to look at Markio, his gaze lingering on the diamonds glistening around Markio's neck, before rising to the Cartier sunglasses on Markio's face.

Markio had no idea what to expect from this distant relative of his. They had met for the first time over a video call earlier this morning. Jarvon had flown from Baton Rouge with Markio's older sister, Taquisha, so Taquisha could visit her son, Tyquan, in the hospital. On the video call, speaking in peculiar Louisiana tongue, Jarvon had explained his situation. He was wanted for questioning concerning several unsolved homicides in Baton Rouge, so he'd volunteered to tag along with Taquisha on her emergency trip to the Midwest. Markio had told him about the federal investigation he himself was going through, and the two of them had seemed to click, binding over a mutual distaste for law enforcement and their mutual love for the streets.

"I read a few chapters from one of your books a couple of months ago, ya heard me?" J-Slime said, his golden smile returning. "Didn't even know you was my kin when I was readin it. I was in East Baton Rouge Parish prison on a parole violation. Only had a few weeks left on parole, so they couldn't do much to me. Sat in my cell and read about half of the second book in that *Bird Man* series. Shit was lit, ya heard me? For real for real."

"Thanks, cuz. I appreciate it."

"Don't call me 'cuz.' I hate that word. Just call me Slime or J-Slime."

Markio thought about it and chuckled. "Cuz" was another name for a Crip, he remembered suddenly, and J-Slime was clearly not one of those.

"So, you a Blood, huh?" Markio asked, an amused smirk playing at the corners of his mouth.

Nodding his head, J-Slime pulled a green bandana from the rear right-hand pocket of his jeans and laid it across his lap. A prideful expression came over his face as he flattened and straightened the large green square of fabric. He nodded again and said, "Been Blood gang all my life. I'm from the north, ya heard me? Slime gang or no gang at all. And I'm Big Slime. Niggas dyin behind this green flag. E'ry nigga done tried us done got whacked or tied up."

"Aww, shit," Apple said, dramatically snatching the ski mask off the top of his head. "We got another you, Lord. Another crazy ass nigga with a pistol. Fuck that. Let me out this van. Pull over right here and let me the fuck out."

Slime cracked up laughing. So did Markio. They poured up Styrofoam cups of cream soda and Wockhardt while Apple recounted the story of how he, Chubb, and Rev had snatched Whitney from the strip club parking lot last night.

Shakia did pull over a few minutes later, but it was only because they'd arrived at the Gucci store. Markio went in with them, and while they shopped around, he put in his AirPods to FaceTime Blubby, a Gangster Disciple with a severe stutter and a notoriously jovial disposition. He'd met Blubby more than two decades ago in Michigan City, Indiana, and they'd been close friends ever since.

Blubby's fat, round face was one large smile when he appeared on the phone screen.

"B-b-but, man, I was just t-talkin about you," he said, rubbing a hand down his face. The corners of his eyes were still crusted with sleep. "L-look where I'm at." Instead of switching to the rear camera, he turned the front of his phone to scan the room. It was a hotel suite. Quez and Snoop, two Four Corner Hustlers who were also from Michigan City, were sitting on the edge of one bed, Snoop snorting a small pyramid of white powder off his pinkie nail, Quez rolling a blunt. Two young, Black women lay in the bed behind them, the blanket pulled up to their bare shoulders in a way that left Markio to believe they were naked beneath it. There were two empty Remy Martin VSOP bottles on the nightstand standing alongside a Ruger handgun, a box of Trojan condoms, and a baggie of round, blue pills.

"B-but, man, we been in here with these two Fort Wayne bitches all night," Blubby said, bringing the camera back to his face. "We was just talkin about you and Whitney. You know they g-g-got her on the news? She got k-k..."

"Yeah, I know," Markio said. "She got kidnapped. I was there when it happened." He was at a clothing rack, checking the size on an off-white Gucci sweater and ignoring the blonde, white store clerk who was lingering a few feet behind him, darting around nervously. "Look, I need you to do me a favor. It's important, bruh. I need you to drive over there to Whitney's house on Comb Street and watch for a white box truck. Park a few houses down and just wait and call me if you see it pull up."

"A'ight. L-let me brush my teeth. I'll be over there in twenty m-m-minutes."

"Yup. Just call me."

Markio pocketed his phone and turned to look at the young, white woman. She was college age, maybe nineteen or twenty, with intelligent, blue eyes and an aquiline nose. She reminded Markio of Charlia, the white girl from TMZ with the annoyingly nasal voice. As soon as he laid eyes on her, she lit up and walked over to him. He was just about to ask her why she was watching him instead of watching their eight other white customers when she beamed a mouthful of braces and pulled out her phone.

"Forgive me if I'm wrong but aren't you the writer from the picture Alexus posted?" she asked. Which caught Markio completely off guard. He'd been under the impression that she was watching him to make sure he didn't steal anything. Before he could reply to the question, she added, "Can I get a picture with you?"

Markio let her take the picture. The girl introduced herself as Amber and gave him a hug. Then, seeing that J-Slime and Shakia — who were in no way related since Shakia was Markio's half-sister on his father's side, while Jarvon was his second cousin on his mother's side — were busy shopping, he tapped Apple on the shoulder, and the two of them went back out to the Sprinter van.

Markio felt his phone buzzing in his pocket as he was settling into his seat. He took it out and saw a new text message from Lil Luke.

"Lord, we on the Ana with the bros. Let me know if you need us. And check out the screenshot. Some old nigga just threatened you on IG. I was about to post in yo comments when I saw it. I showed the gang. Don't nobody know that nigga."

The "Ana" was 16th Street and Christiana Avenue, the block where younger TVLs hung out in Markio's west side neighborhood.

Markio touched the screenshot and zoomed in on the comments. @BossBreed1300 had posted. "Bitch ass nigga." Then, "We gon catch all you hoe ass Travelers one by one." And finally, "Steel Toe home now, lil nigga! Y'ALL KILLED MY SON!! On Black Gangsta, I'm on y'all ass! I bet not c dat Rolls Royce truck nowhere! I BET I flip dat mufucka!"

Underneath that last comment, Lil Luke had replied. "Get off the Internet with this police ass shit. Pull up. We on Christiana right now."

Markio furrowed his brow and went to @BossBreed1300's page, only to find that it was set to private. All he could see was the profile picture, which showed an older looking, Black man with a graying shadow of a beard and a bald head. He had no idea who the man was, but judging from the man's Instagram name, Markio figured he might be a Black Gangster New Breed from somewhere on 13th Street.

He went to his own Instagram page and found that the man had already deleted the threatening comments. Markio was glad to see them gone. The last thing he needed was a man threatening him in his comments and then turning up dead a few hours later. Which was likely to happen.

There were more than five million followers on Markio's page, and he had the little blue checkmark by his name. Most of his followers came from people wanting to see the man Nikkia Staples was dating; her page had forty-two million followers. Another million of Markio's followers had appeared after Nikkia's close friend, Alexus Costilla, posted a photo that showed Alexus standing next to Markio inside the Versace mansion in Miami Beach, Florida.

With well over four hundred million followers and a reported net worth of $228 billion, Alexus Costilla had surpassed Selena Gomez and Kylie Jenner to become the most followed female celebrity on Instagram, and she was also the second wealthiest person on the planet, with only a mere one billion dollars keeping her from taking Elon Musk's number one spot. It was Alexus who'd streamlined the movie deal Markio had signed just yesterday, a deal that had put $10 million in his checking account and guaranteed that his bestselling book series would hit the big screen in a very big way. It was Alexus' Mexican drug cartel that had sold him two thousand pounds of exotic marijuana, two hundred kilos of fish scale cocaine, fifty kilos of uncut Mexican heroin, and fifty kilos of pure fentanyl. It also didn't hurt that Alexus had married Blake "Bulletface" King, the first real gangsta rapper to become an official billionaire.

A sudden rustling of plastic caused Markio to look up from his phone screen. Apple was tearing the wrapper off a chocolate-covered honey bun. He took a huge bite out of it and, while chewing, said, "Text Shakia. Tell her to come out here…. and turn on this heat… before we fuck around and freeze in this bitch."

Markio chuckled and shook his head. "Let that honey bun warm you up," he said and chuckled again. "You know a nigga they call Steel Toe or some'n like that? I think he might be one of the Breeds. A older nigga."

Apple shook his head no. "Ain't never heard of no nigga named Steel Toe." He took another bite. He chewed and swallowed. "I know Breed Steel who just got out the joint the other day. Cash Boy's uncle."

"That might be him. Who is Cash Boy?"

Apple shrugged his shoulders. "Some lil nigga off Sawyer they wacked a couple of years ago. His boy got killed with him. I think Jah knocked them niggas off right after he got married to ol' sexy ass Tirzah. They say Cash Boy had some words with Tirzah at a gas station and ended up putting his hands on her. Next thing we know, he was dead. They say he ain't last three hours after he put his hands on Tirzah."

Markio stuck out his bottom lip and nodded his head. He'd been in prison a couple of years ago. He'd never even heard of Cash Boy, and Jah was a kid when Markio went to prison. But none of that mattered now. Steel had made the critical mistake of threatening a real life gangster, and Markio wasn't going to rest until the old man was six feet underground.

Chapter 4

Twenty-year-old Simon "Skip" Newsome was sitting on the toilet with a long, hard log of shit sliding out from his asshole and one forefinger jammed up his nostril when his older brother, Bryshere "Pojo" Newsome, kicked open the locked bathroom door.

"You stole those ten dollars off my dresser," Pojo snarled. He took one step forward, his six-foot, two-hundred-pound frame filling the doorway.

Stunned by the violent intrusion, Skip looked up. He almost blurted out a defensive lie. Then, his stunned expression morphed into a contemptuous scowl, and he said, "You goddamn right I took it. You and Elise got all drunk last night, wrestling around and shit, and ended up spilling orange juice all over my fucking cigarettes. I had just paid eighteen goddamn dollars for them Newports. Hadn't even smoked two squares. Shit, y'all owe me eight mo dollars."

"That was gas money for Elise to get to work," Pojo said snappishly. "Ol bitch ass nigga."

"Nigga, I wouldn't give a fuck if it was money for cancer treatment," Skip snapped back. The force of his words caused his sphincter to snap shut, pinching off the turd and sending it splashing down into the toilet water beneath him. "Y'all wet up my whole pack of cigarettes. I needed another pack, so I took that ten dollars and went and bought me another motherfucking pack. And I don't give a fuck who mad about it."

Fuming, Pojo snatched off his faded, blue t-shirt and threw it into the hallway behind him. "I'm beating yo ass when you get off that toilet," he said and stormed out of the bathroom.

"You got me fucked up if you think I'ma keep letting you punch on me," Skip shouted after him. He started wiping his ass, thinking of the .380 caliber Mac 12 submachine gun he had in his bedroom closet and wishing he'd had the foresight to bring it to the bathroom with him.

He had never won a fight against Pojo. Skip was a full four inches shorter and sixty pounds lighter than his twenty-two-year-old brother, and Pojo was great at using his size to his advantage. They'd had several bloody fist fights in the eight months since they first moved into the cramped, two-bedroom apartment. The apartment building was on 13th and Keeler, in an area of North Lawndale where dozens of their fellow New Breeds could be found at all times of the day. The gang had already broken up three serious brawls between the two unruly brothers, the last of which took place on Halloween night and had left Skip with a fractured eye socket.

"I'm tellin' you right now, Pojo," Skip hollered as he wrapped his hand with toilet paper for another wipe, "if you swing on me when I get out there, I'm shooting yo ass. I'ma shoot you and Elise. And I'ma tell Mama why I did it. Both of y'all got me…"

Skip's empty threats came to an abrupt halt as Pojo came rushing in through the open doorway. Skip ducked his head just in time to dodge a potential knockout blow to the temple. He closed his arms around Pojo's waist and held on tight as he was lifted off the toilet. He grimaced at the pain of two hard punches to the ribs. Realizing he needed to get his gym shorts and boxers from around his ankles before he could even hope to launch a counterattack, he quickly kicked out of them and then pushed away from Pojo.

For a second or two, they stood, facing each other with their fists raised in front of them, Skip naked from the waist down, Pojo bare skinned from the waist up. Pojo's girlfriend, Elise, stood in the doorway in her Target uniform, hands on her hips, her flashy dark-skinned face scrunched into an evil glare. Someone's phone began to ring in another room, and Elise must've been expecting a call because she turned and hurried away two seconds before the real action got underway.

Pojo faked a kick, Skip moved to avoid it, and Pojo's right hand shot out in a lightning-fast jab that caught Skip right on the mouth. He threw a wild punch that slammed into Pojo's jaw, but it didn't inflict much damage. Pojo's quick hands came at him in a flurry, popping his face with solid blows that dazed him and sent him into a defensive crouch, and once again, he found himself with his arms wrapped around Pojo's waist. This time, Pojo put him in an under armed headlock, and as his big brother's arm tightened around his neck, completely cutting off his air supply, he panicked and tried punching Pojo in the nuts.

And when that didn't work, he reached into the toilet bowl and clasped his hand around that fat log of shit he'd pushed out a minute earlier.

The turd was wet and slimy in his hand. Pojo must have seen him grab it because he let go of Skip's neck and tried to jump back.

But it was too late. Skip's hand was already in motion. He looked up and saw pure dread in his older brother's eyes as an immense wave of victory washed over him. With the turd essentially glued to his open palm, he slapped Pojo hard across the face. The log of shit landed diagonally from the right corner of Pojo's mouth all the way up to his left eye. It smashed against his face and, for the most part, stayed there with only a couple of sticking chunks dropping wetly to the tiled bathroom floor.

The fight ended right then and there. Pojo doubled over and vomited. Skip left the bathroom without retrieving his boxers and gym shorts, and when he ran into Elise in the hallway, holding Pojo's phone to her ear and telling someone that Skip had stolen her gas money, he slapped her with the same hand he'd used to slap Pojo, leaving a wet brown handprint across the side of her pudgy, black face.

"Stupid ass bitch," he said, glowering at Elise as she fell back against the wall and crumbled to the floor. "I'm shit slapping you bitches from here on out. Every time one of you niggas get outta line with me, I'ma shit slap the fuck out of you."

Elise brought her hand up to touch the fetid slime on her face, and then, she vomited too, right there on the hallway floor. The Samsung smartphone tumbled out of her hand and landed face up. Skip saw his mother's phone number on the screen. The call was still going, so he picked up the phone and went into his bedroom.

"Yo son gon make me kill him and that fat ass werewolf he call a girlfriend," Skip said, lifting a dirty sock from the floor and using it to wipe some of the shit off his hand. He pulled on a pair of grey sweatpants and went to his closet to grab his Mac 12 off the high shelf.

"You fucking dumbasses," Neetra said, her voice coming through the speaker loud and clear as Pojo's phone lay screen up on Skip's unmade bed. "While you and Pojo are over there fighting over ten funky ass dollars, I'm sitting here with five thousand dollars your uncle wants me to pay y'all to go over there and drop one of them boys who killed y'all's brother."

That got Skip's attention. It was not just the five grand but also the idea of sliding on the opps who'd murdered his oldest brother, Durron, almost seven years ago. Although Skip was just thirteen when it happened, he and Pojo had already been blessed into the New Breed gang, and they'd wasted no time earning their stripes by avenging their brother's death. Skip had caught a Traveler riding a bike through the alley on 13th a few days later, and using the .38 caliber revolver his gang's chief, Dana "Bird" Boston, had given him, he'd shot the boy twice in the back and four times in the back of his head. Three days after that, he and Pojo caught another Traveler walking out of a girl's house on Kedvale. The boy had spotted them and took off running, but they'd chased after him and gunned him down in the intersection of 13th Street and Sawyer Avenue. The war went on for years and had only calmed down when most of the shooters were either killed or sent to prison, but there was still tension. There would always be tension. The main reason why all the gang members were so focused on finessing and trapping their way to a fortune was so they could be ready for summertime when the streets heated up again.

The five grand was exactly what Skip needed to get his money up. He knew a Mickey Cobra from the low end who sold fake Percocets for the low. He just needed the money to cop some, and he'd be able to quadruple his investment in a matter of weeks or maybe even days.

He could hear Elise crying in the bathroom. Someone had turned on the shower. "It is either him or me!" Elise was yelling, and it didn't sound like Pojo was saying anything back.

"Shit, Mama," Skip said, picking up the phone and throwing the Mac 12's shoulder strap over his head. "I'ma let you try to talk this nigga, Pojo, into slidin' with me. He a lil mad at me right now."

Chapter 5

"We need to be in Chicago, knocking on doors and asking people if they've seen our fucking mother, not sitting here on our asses in Michigan City, giving the niggas who kidnapped her all the time in the fucking world to do whatever the fuck they feel like doing to her."

No one replied to seventeen-year-old Eva Clarrett's ill-tempered rant. She was pacing back and forth across the pink carpeted living room floor with tears in her eyes, her fists balled up at her sides. Ava, Eva's identical twin sister was sitting on her boyfriend Flocka's lap on their new hot pink, leather sectional sofa. Their fifteen-year-old sister, Joselyn, sat at the opposite end of the sofa, both legs drawn up beneath her, her pretty hazel eyes red-rimmed from all the crying she'd done since news broke of their mother's kidnapping.

Eva stopped pacing and grabbed her hips. She looked from Joselyn to Flocka, and her gaze lingered on him for a short moment. He was a tall, athletically built nineteen-year-old with long dreadlocks and a somewhat handsome, dark brown face. Eva had fucked him several times behind her twin sister's back. She'd initially planned to make it a one time thing, but he had a long tongue, and he'd used it to both lick inside her pussy and lick all over her clitoris. Then, after making her cum two times in a row, he'd wriggled that talented tongue of his deep into her asshole. He was a nasty lover, and Eva loved nasty. He had a big dick too, but it was his tongue that had her sprung. So, she'd gone back to him for seconds. And thirds. And early this morning, fourths.

"There's nothing we can do in Chicago that we can't do from here," Ava said after a long bout of silence. "Plus, it's just not safe to be knocking on people's doors out there. They say that neighborhood Mama got taken from is way too dangerous. It's where that cop and three other people got killed the other day."

"I know," said Eva. "It's Markio old neighborhood. He was there at the strip club when Mama got kidnapped last night, and I find it really fucking funny that he hasn't called to check on `us."

Eva's iPhone rang in the back pocket of her skintight, blue jeans. She pulled it out and saw that it was her mother's boyfriend, Voltaire, calling. Two seconds later, someone blew their horn out front.

Sniffling, Eva thumbed the tears from her eyes and answered the FaceTime call, walking to the picture window to look out through the hot pink, venetian blinds that overlooked their front yard. Voltaire appeared on her phone screen, and, peeking through the horizontal slats, she saw that it was him who'd blown the horn. He was in a box truck. A white one. His arrival brought a huge sense of relief to Eva. Voltaire had a strong dominant aura about him that made her feel safe and invincible in his presence.

"I'm outside," he said in this thick, Haitian accent. Eva sensed a thinly veiled pain in his eyes. He was obviously hurting, and she felt compelled to go out and comfort him.

"I'm coming out now," she said and ended the call. She looked at Ava. "Voltaire just pulled up. Let me go out here and talk to him," Eva said, picking up her bag of Skittles from the coffee table.

Leaving the room, she intentionally added a seductive swing to her hips, knowing that Flocka would undoubtedly be watching. Like most men, he couldn't help it. The Clarrett twins were every man's dream, two thickly built redbones with gorgeous faces, barely there waistlines, and fat, bouncy asses that seemed to jiggle with every step they took. Eva and Ava dropped jaws everywhere they went. Their younger sister, Joselyn, was just as stunning and even thicker below the waist, so maturely developed that most men she encountered thought she was much older than her fifteen years.

Eva pulled the hood of her white, iKiss Kosmetics hoodie up over her head and went out the front door. The air was cold, crisp, and welcoming. She inhaled deeply, filling her lungs with it as she started down the porch steps, glancing left at Michigan Boulevard's sparse morning traffic. And to think, just yesterday, she'd been absorbing the humid warmth of South Florida, lounging around the Olympic sized pool outside Voltaire's brother, Keondre's palatial Miami Beach mansion.

Coated in a thin layer of snow, the cherry red Honda Accord her mother had left to them sat parked outside their chain-link fence. The twins had given the car to Joselyn and used the $50,000 Whitney wired them a week before Christmas to purchase their own vehicles, two blood red Jeep Grand Cherokees. They owed on the trucks, but the lump sums they'd put down on them made for low monthly payments, and with the thousands of dollars Whitney sent to them every other week, they could more than afford it. The two Jeeps were parked behind Joselyn's Honda, and Voltaire's big, white box truck was idling in the middle of the street, smoke from the exhaust pipe billowing up from its rear end.

Eva dumped a bunch of Skittles in her mouth and climbed in next to him. She looked him up and down as she reached out to pull the door shut. God, he was handsome. He had long dreadlocks like Flocka, only his were thick, like tree branches. He sported a diamond wristwatch and a diamond Cuban-link necklace. A gray Ralph Lauren sweatshirt with a matching skullcap. Blue designer jeans and fresh gray Nike

Dunks. He both smelled and looked like money, and when he leaned in toward Eva, she planted a soft, sucky kiss on his thick, black lips and thought, *Damn, he even tastes like money.*

"Pull off," she said, worried that one of her sisters might look out the front window and uncover the secret she knew would shatter their mother's heart to pieces.

She'd been flirting with Voltaire from the moment she walked in and saw him working out in Keondre's spacious indoor fitness center. He'd been lying on his back, bare chested and sweaty, bench pressing over three hundred pounds worth of circular steel plates, and she'd said something like, "Mmm, boy, let me kiss on that six pack." She hadn't thought anything would come of it. But then, shortly after Whitney and her friend, Bunny, left to apply some finishing touches to the first brick and mortar iKiss Kosmetics store before its grand opening, he'd caught Eva in the kitchen, bending over in the fridge to reach for a cold bottle of Figi water, and he'd pressed up on her from behind. She'd turned around and tongue kissed him for a good twenty seconds., allowing his powerful, black hands to roam and squeeze all over her bountiful round ass, and she'd left him standing there with a tent in the front of his shorts.

They had kissed again at the iKiss store, a quick five second tongue battle in the employee's restroom while Whitney was busy in her office, but they hadn't taken it any further than that. Eva had decided not to. Voltaire was a fine ass nigga, and clearly a rich one too, but he belonged to her mother, and she knew that looking herself in the mirror would be a nearly impossible task if she went all the way with him.

He made a U-turn and was approaching Michigan Boulevard when Eva looked in the sideview mirror and saw Blubby's dark blue Volkswagen Atlas. It was the 2023 model, and it sat high above a sparkling gold set of Forgiato rims. She knew it was Blubby's truck because, like everyone else in her city, she kept track of all the niggas who were getting money. Blubby sold exotic weed, everything from grams to ounces and pounds, and the word on the street was that Markio was his plug. He was parked across the street and three houses down, but it was clearly him, and maybe Eva's eyes were playing tricks on her, but it looked to her like he'd had his smartphone raised over the steering wheel, as if he was snapping a photo or recording video of the box truck she was in.

"So," she asked Voltaire, "can you tell me anything about what might've happened to my mama? Anything. I mean, I'm almost eighteen. I'm grown enough to hear the truth."

"Which way do I turn?" Voltaire looked left and right, and then, his eyes settled on the huge police station perched atop the hill, just across the boulevard. "Shit, the police are right there. I could not live here. Not on this street."

Eva giggled lightly. "Turn right," she said, taking out her phone.

Voltaire made the turn and drove northbound down Michigan Boulevard. Several blocks down, Eva instructed him to make a left turn that took them across the boulevard and onto East 10th Street. They passed Petty's convenience store on their right, and then, Eva had him make a right turn into the alleyway just behind the store. He went about halfway down the alley and stopped, pulling over next to a ramshackle garage behind an abandoned home.

He turned and looked over at Eva. He sighed through his nose and pressed one large hand against his face. Eva was checking the views on her and Ava's most recent TikTok video. It showed the two of them twerking in booty shorts to the beat of Latto and GloRilla's *FTCU* song, and it was already up to eighty-nine thousand views.

"I lost three of my young boys yesterday and two more a little bit ago," Voltaire said. He sounded emotional. Grief stricken. "And then, on top of that, I have no idea who has your mother."

Eva gawked at him, stunned by the revelation. "What do you mean you *lost* them? Like, they died?"

He nodded. "It was the ex-boy. Markio. His people. They killed three of my Zoes. Then, two more OD'ed on me a little over an hour ago, on the southside of Chicago. And now, my boy, Woppo, ain't answering. I got a bad feeling. A bad, bad feeling."

"Does that have anything to do with what happened to Mama?"

Voltaire hesitated. Then, "I'm not sure. Maybe so. We took the ex-boy for some things, and I think he may be a little upset about it."

"Someone was watching us," said Eva.

"Just now?" he asked.

"Yeah. Just a minute ago. One of Markio's boys. He was parked up the street in that dark blue truck with the gold rims. That's Dub Life Blubby."

Both Voltaire and Eva shot quick glances at their sideview mirrors. Eva found her view obstructed by a row of hedges that jutted out from beside the neighboring garage, but she could see enough to capture a fleeting glimpse of a blue SUV as it drove past the mouth of the alleyway and continued up 10th Street. She only saw its rear end, but she was almost certain it was Blubby's.

"I need somewhere safe to park this truck," Voltaire said. He pulled a long-bladed machete from behind his seat and placed it in the panel of his door. "A safe place the ex-boy doesn't know about. I have... expensive cargo. Can't just leave this anywhere."

"We can park it at my Aunt Candace's house. She'll be in Miami running the store at least until we find Mama. Or we could..."

Eva's words became frozen in her throat as she looked forward and saw Blubby's SUV cruise to a stop at the far end of the alleyway directly ahead of them. There was a thin-faced man in the passenger's seat. He reminded Eva of Snoop Dogg.

"Oh, my God. That's them. That's Blubby's truck right there," she said.

But Voltaire was already on it. He reached to the left side, and for a moment, Eva though he was going for the machete. Then, his hand came up holding an AR style pistol with a banana clip and a long, black silencer screwed into its barrel, and he threw open his door just as Blubby was maneuvering his big blue SUV to turn into the alley.

Eva gasped. Voltaire leaned out a little, positioned the AR pistol so that its silencer was sticking out between his doorframe, and squeezed off a rapid burst of ammunition that left more than a dozen holes stitched across the hood and windshield of Blubby's sleek blue Volkswagon Atlas. Eva thought she saw the gaunt faced passenger jerk in his seat as Blubby frantically spun the steering wheel and raced off down the side street.

Eva slid down in her seat, her innocent, young mind in shambles. She went to Google Maps on her phone and typed in the address to her Aunt Candace's home in the Deep Lakeland neighborhood of Michigan City, then she handed the phone to Voltaire and hunkered down as he stomped on the gas pedal and sent the box truck barreling up the snow-laden alleyway, rocking side to side on its rickety suspension.

Lord, please let me make it back home, Eva prayed, interlacing her fingers beneath her chin. *I'll stop being a thot right now and go to church every Sunday if you just let me make it back home to my family.*

Chapter 6

"A'ight, sis. Drive safe," Markio said and slapped the hood of Shakia's shiny, black Jeep Compass before she drove off down the long, serpentine driveway that led up to the front of Nikkia's opulent Greystone Burr Ridge mansion.

He turned around and, with his head lowered against the frigid breeze, hurried into the open sliding door of Nikkia's six car garage. Apple was in the driver's seat of Markio's snow-white Rolls Royce Cullinan, adjusting it to his liking. J-Slime was in the backseat, and when Markio got in beside him, he saw that his distant cousin was on a FaceTime call with a little girl who couldn't have been any more than three or four years old.

"Daddy love you," J-Slime was saying to the cute little toddler.

"I love you!" she replied sweetly.

And suddenly, Markio was thinking of his own daughter, who was currently growing in the belly of the beautiful Mya Patterson. Mya, a twenty-two-year-old elite real estate agent and the sister of multimillionaire drug kingpin Leroy "Bam" Patterson Jr., had recently moved back to Chicago in a luxurious Gold Coast high-rise condominium that cost her $7,200 a month. Markio had only learned of her pregnancy last night while he was seated at a table with Bam and some other high-ranking TVLs in the VIP section at Redbone's Gentleman's Club. She'd FaceTimed Bam, and he'd handed his phone to Markio. A short while later (and mere minutes

42

after he'd had his childhood friends, Apple, Rev, and Chubb, snatch Whitney from the parking lot), Markio has sent his younger cousin, Tito, to drop off a rubber banded pile of hundreds to Mya at her condo. $100,000. More than enough to pay up her mortgage for the year, freeing up her personal income for the baby she was due to have three months from now.

But now was no time to be thinking about Mya and the child they were expecting. Markio brought out his two iPhones and used his prepaid trap phone to place a FaceTime call to Blubby, sticking both of his AirPods in his ears to block out J-Slime's phone conversation. He didn't even look up as Apple drove out of the garage and down the driveway. He had a lot on his mind. Two of his closest cousins, Kay and Buck, were sitting in Cook County jail, charged with a murder they'd done for him. He and Bam had almost gone to war over that murder because the victim was Bam's (and Mya's) nephew, Binky. His own nephew, Tyquan, who was currently hospitalized with two gunshot wounds to the chest, was also under arrest for possession of more than two thousand pounds of high-grade marijuana and twelve kilograms of fentanyl that had belonged to him. And now, there was the added trouble of having to deal with Steel and whoever he had on his team. But at the moment, Markio's only focus was recovering his missing bricks of cocaine, heroin, and fentanyl. Everything else could wait.

The phone line rang and rang and rang in Markio's ears. He'd FaceTimed with Blubby a few minutes ago. He'd witnessed the shocking kiss between Voltaire and one of Whitney's twin daughters (Markio could never tell Eva and Ava apart), and he'd had the mind to screenshot the image before the kiss ended. Voltaire had made a U-turn and pulled off in the box truck a moment later. Blubby said he was going to follow them, and then, the call dropped.

Now, Blubby wasn't picking up, and Markio didn't have Snoop's number.

He ended his attempt at contacting Blubby and poured some Wockhardt and Sprite over the ice cubes in his Styrofoam cup. The Lean was starting to make his gut stick out a bit more than he was used to, but he enjoyed the high promethazine with codeine syrup gave him too much to give it up.

J-Slime spoke with the mother of his daughter for a couple of minutes, sure not to bring up the cash he'd gotten from Markio but promising to wire her a thousand dollars for their daughter as soon as he transferred the money to his card.

"What she got? Cash App?" Markio asked. "Zelle? PayPal?"

J-Slime looked at him and shook his head. "You did enough already, fam. She got Cash App, but I'll send her the bread out my money."

"Nah, I got a few racks for her. Just tell me how to send it," Markio said, and he watched the elated smile spread across the pretty, Black woman's face as Jarvon gave him her Cash App number. He sent her $4,500.00, placing his phone on the armrest next to him, so Jarvon could see the transaction, and she immediately yelped with joy.

"Tell him I said thank you!" she exclaimed.

"Just make sure you spend half of that on my daughter," J-Slime said tightly. She promised she would. Slime ended the call and put fire to the blunt he'd rolled while Markio was on the phone with Blubby.

"You ain't have to do that, fam," Slime said, his voice sounding creaky due to the smoke he was holding in. "You already gave me ten when I got in the van with you, and your lil sister spent another nine on this jacket. That's nineteen racks. I appreciate it, but I ain't come out here for that, ya heard me. I just wanted to get out of Louisiana for a lil minute and meet my people, ya heard me? That's it. That's all."

"And you met me. This what I do, run the bag up and spend it on my people. In the past six months, I done spent over two million, and half of that went to my family and the gang. If it ain't about them, it ain't about nothin.'"

"Ha haaa. I like that, five," said Slime, his gold teeth glimmering as he smiled and blew smoke out of his nose. He looked much better than he had when they first picked him up from the train stop. He was wearing the black leather Gucci jacket Shakia had bought for him over a black and green Gucci jogger and black leather Gucci sneakers. He'd taken a quick shower in the mansion before changing into his more expensive attire, and he seemed a lot happier now, less cautious, and more comfortable in Markio's presence.

He took a long pull from the blunt, passed it over to Markio, and in that creaky, smoky lunged tone of voice asked, "So, what we on, five?" Keeping his iPhone on the leather armrest between them, Markio went to Whitney's Instagram page and pressed play on a video that showed Voltaire and Denver Broncos' star running back Keondre Muck in a pull-up competition.

"That's Keondre Muck," Slime said, pointing.

Markio nodded and pointed at the second man in the video. "And that's his brother, Voltaire, the nigga who got my bricks. He gon die if I don't get 'em back. Matter of fact, he gon die either way it go, but it's gon be a closed casket funeral if I don't get my shit back."

"You know where to find him?"

"Yup. Just saw him on FaceTime." Markio went to the screenshot and zoomed in on the scandalous smooch. "That's him kissing on one of his girlfriend's daughters in front of her house in Michigan City. He got my bricks in the back of that box truck."

Slime rose in his seat and reached over into the rear storage compartment. He grabbed his new Gucci duffle bag and opened it on his lap. Inside of it was a mini-Draco AK-47 pistol that Markio had given him while they were inside the mansion, as well as the other new clothes he'd purchased at Gucci, and the outfit he'd had on earlier. He lifted out the mini-Draco and stared longingly at it, as if it were a sexy stripper and not a deadly, fully automatic weapon.

"You already know how I'm rockin', ya heard me?" Slime said, his slow Southern drawl somehow managing to sound both gritty and energetic. "It's northside, thirty-eighth. We put guns to the face. Who gon die today?"

Markio had heard that exact same slogan in a rap song recently. He squinted his eyes, struggling to remember it as he toked on the blunt and coughed up a storm, and he was seconds away from naming the song when the iPhone he used to talk with his family and conduct legitimate business rang with a call from a number with a 219 area code. Which meant the caller was either from Gary, Hammond, East Chicago, or Michigan City. He knew a lot of people in those northwest Indiana cities, but only a few of them had his personal number.

He accepted the call but waited for the person on the other end to speak.

"Hello? Is this Markio?" It was a young, Black woman's voice.

"Yeah," Markio said. "This him. Who is this?"

The caller sighed through the phone. "Do you know where we can find my mama?" she asked, and Markio immediately recognized her voice. It was one of Whitney's obscenely gorgeous twin daughters, either Eva or Ava.

"Nah, I ain't heard from her." He put the call on speaker and placed the phone on the armrest. "Who is this? Eva?"

"It's Ava. Eva just left with Voltaire. I don't know where they went, but she'll be back soon. She hated riding with other people ever since we got those Jeeps. She seems to think you might know something about what happened to Mama. Because you and her were both there at that strip club, you know? And because she was taken in your old neighborhood."

"I don't know what the fuck happened," Markio lied. He took a sip of Lean and a puff of gelato. "The shit went down so fast. I was just walkin out the club. Somebody screamed, and then, that Avalanche was speedin out the parking lot. She was with Bunny and Brandon when that shit went down. You better off askin them what happened."

"I figured you didn't know anything. I told Joselyn you and Mama might've broken up or whatever, but you always loved her and showed her the utmost respect, and you loved us like you was our real daddy. I knew you didn't have nothin' to do with it."

"Hell nawl, I ain't have nothing to do with it. I'm on top of it though. Soon as I hear something, I'll let you know. Text Eva and ask her where she at. I'm on my way out there now, and I wanna surprise her."

"Okay. I'll just call her and then call you back."

After the call with Ava, Markio sat, staring out his window and thinking. As much as he hated to admit it, he really did love Whitney, almost as much as he loved Nikkia. He thought about what Apple had told him about Chubb and Rev looking like they were going to rape Whitney before he left out. The mental image of Whitney being hurt or raped by one of Markio's own homeboys tightened his lungs more than any puff of weed ever could.

He picked up his trap phone and called Rev.

Chapter 7

Whitney Clarrett's throat ached from all the muted screaming she'd done over the past half hour, and she was pretty sure she'd blacked out at least twice. But the blackouts weren't enough. She wanted to die. The fiery waves of pain emanating from her stomach were too much to bear.

She'd been fine with the fat guy and his bigfoot penis. He'd stretched her open wider than she'd ever been stretched by any man, but that pain had been a good pain, a pain she felt she could endure for months on end. He'd let her shower afterwards, and when he brought her back to the large, square room, he'd raped her again, holding his gun against the side of her neck. She'd seen that either he or Gray Mask had mopped up the puddle of urine she'd left on the floor.

Then, Gray Mask had taken his turn with her, bending her over an old, brown armchair and fucking her from behind. His dick was nowhere as large as the fat guy's, but it was just as long, and he had a lot of stamina. He'd fucked her for a solid twenty minutes before spilling his seed in his condom, and then, he and the fat guy had duct taped her to another wooden chair, this time making her sit naked, facing the rear, with her ass hanging over the front of the seat. Gray Mask handled her roughly during the retaping, which had made her feel a bit fearful of his intentions.

But never had she expected this.

Gray Mask had, for some evil fucking reason, slipped a cold, steel curling iron into her pussy from behind. She'd gasped at the coldness of the steel inside her warm, wet hole. Then, he'd plugged the curling iron into the power socket, and Whitney's eyes had bulged out of their sockets as the cold steel became hotter and hotter. Then, she began to throw her weight around on the chair in a fruitless attempt to get it out of her. She'd howled deep in her throat, like a wounded hound, and then, she'd blacked out. When she regained consciousness, the iron was out of her, and Gray Mask had one hand clamped tight around the front of her neck while he yelled obscenities in her ear.

"You wanna set niggas up! Huh, bitch?! You wanna set up robberies and shit! You stupid ass bitch!"

Saliva had splattered her earlobe and the side of her neck. Gray Mask's fist had slammed down hard against the back of her head, bringing tiny, little, black spots into her vision, and then, he'd rammed the curling iron back into her and plugged it back into the power socket. She'd blacked out again, but when she came to, the iron was still in her. She felt the intense heat of the hot steel cooking things inside of her that weren't meant to be cooked. The putrid stench of burnt flesh permeated the basement air. It became so overpowering that Black Mask lifted the neckline of his designer sweater to cover his nose. Whitney's wide, teary eyes were on him when he did it, and some part of her brain registered the tattoo arced across his fat, hanging belly. MAFIA INSANE, it read in large, capital lettering.

Relief only came when Gray Mask's phone rang a few infinite seconds later. He snatched the curling iron out of her, along with some burnt bits of flesh, and walked off to the utility closet to answer the call. Whitney hung her head over the back of the chair and wept uncontrollably, her body trembling from scalp to heel.

God, please, she prayed with all the faith in her possession. *Just let me die. Just take me now. I can't take it anymore…*

Chapter 8

"What's the word, Lord?" Baby Lord said as soon as the collect jail call came through.

Lil Luke grinned at the unbridled excitement he heard in his best friend, Baby Lord's voice. He was sitting in the driver's seat of his blacked-out, 2019 Dodge Charger Hellcat, parked in the alleyway on 15th and Christiana. Big Keanan's Challenger Hellcat was parked right behind the Charger, but none of the gang was outside with Lil Luke. Everyone had gone inside 1527 South Christiana Avenue to kick it with Pig, the gangsta girl who'd had the exotic weed game in their neighborhood on lock for the past five years.

"They finally gave me a bond," Baby Lord said. "But it's a million dollars cash. Ain't nobody in my family got that kinda money. They got me in the hole now, but I should be out in the next few days."

"Wait, what you in the hole for?"

"Had to whoop one of these GDs. Some nigga they call Bishop. Bitch ass nigga ran in my cell and tried to rob me for my commissary. I took off on buddy ass right then and there. Put him straight to sleep."

Lil Luke clenched his teeth and flared his nostrils. His fingers tightened around the handle of the Glock on his lap. "Find out where he from, bruh. I'm slidin on his people. Ain't no fuck nigga finna get away with tryna rob my nigga."

Baby Lord let out an animated chuckle. "It ain't even that serious, bro. Buddy ain't no shit. I'm tryna see if my lawyer can get me a bond reduction, so I can see the streets again."

"You might not even need to do that. I'ma try to holla at Markio. You know they call that nigga Millionaire Markio now? He just got a movie deal with MTN Studios, and he been dropping books left and right. On Neal, bro got a bag. And he been fuckin on that badass lawyer, Nikkia Staples. We just slid on a nigga for bro not even a hour ago. I'ma hit him up and see if he can get you outta there."

Baby Lord laughed joyfully. "Hell yeah. Hit that nigga up right now. Bam might put up the other half if Markio put up the rest. I'll call you back in like twenty minutes."

"A'ight, just hit me."

The call ended, and Lil Luke sat there, smiling for a moment, nodding his head with his dreads swaying and his eyes raking back and forth across the alleyway. If there was one thing he knew about the criminal justice system, it was that money talked. His big homie, Juice, had spent over a hundred thousand dollars on lawyer fees to get him out of prison. He'd been sentenced to life plus fifty-five years in the Illinois Department of Corrections, but he'd served less than five years before his sentence was overturned. Juice, Bam, and Markio were like brothers to one another, and they were like older brothers to the younger members of the gang. Lil Luke knew that with all the millions in drug money the three high-ranking gang leaders had between them, they would not hesitate to put up the cash to get Baby Lord out of jail.

Especially since Bam's now deceased brother, Worm, was the whole reason Baby Lord had gotten charged with the murder in the first place.

Reclining in his seat, Lil Luke spent a few minutes lusting over Noesha Long, a bad, yellow bone he'd been stalking on Instagram for the past couple of weeks. She was a sexy, young baddie with pretty, green eyes, wide hips, thick thighs, and a big, bubble butt she loved showing off to her many hundreds of followers. The girls in her clique — her slender sister, Niecy, and their close friends, Quita, Lacey, Nya, and Brielle — were the same way — bad, young, Black women in their late teens and early twenties with flat stomachs, cute faces, and fat, round asses.

But in Lil Luke's opinion, none of them had anything on Noesha.

He "liked" a couple of her photos, fantasized over a couple of her videos, and left Instagram to text the man half the neighborhood had started calling Millionaire Markio. He'd only typed in seven words — "Bro, jus got off da line wit" — when the low rumble of tires over the small pebbles that littered the redbrick alleyway grabbed his attention.

He sat up a little and turned to peer between his front seats, and what he saw made him duck low, drop his phone, and pick up the Glock from his lap.

It was a burgundy Oldsmobile sedan. It was roughly four car lengths behind him and approaching fast. There was an unattractive, fat faced woman in the driver's seat, her eyes focused on the side of the alley where Pig's house stood. The two men (at least Lil Luke assumed they were men) in the backseat behind her had black ski masks pulled down over their heads, and one of them was holding up what looked like some sort of Mac submachine pistol.

Wasting no time, Lil Luke threw open his door and bailed out with his Glock raised and aimed at the sedan's front windshield. The fat girl's eyes went wide with fear, and so did the two sets of eyes in the ski masks. It was all they had time to do before Lil Luke squeezed the trigger.

Chapter 9

His Austrian-made Glock switch took over after that, spewing out fifteen rounds per second and punching hole after hole through the windshield. The fat girl moved toward her door, pushing it open. One of the boys in the backseat did the same thing, even as numerous 9-millimeter rounds pierced his muscular torso.

Lil Luke was uncertain as to whether he'd wounded the second masked man; the shooting transpired too rapidly for his drug muddled brain to register it all, and as soon as his thirty-shot clip was empty, he was back inside his Charger Hellcat, jetting off down the alleyway and veering onto 16th Street, coming within inches of T-boning a shiny, new Cadillac coupe.

A line of heroin addicts one block over on Spaulding had scattered at the jarring claps of gunfire, several of them sprinting past Lil Luke's car as he slid to a stop to avoid colliding with the Cadillac. He reached down to scoop up his phone from the floorboard. He spun the steering wheel and raced off down 16th, phoning Big Keanan as he did it and checking his rearview mirror just as the Oldsmobile shot out of the alleyway and careened onto 16th Street, heading in the opposite direction.

Lil Luke glimpsed some frantic commotion in the backseat of that fleeing Oldsmobile. Then, his eyes were back on the road ahead as he ejected the depleted magazine from his pistol and snatched another one from his glove compartment.

Big Keanan answered the call with clear urgency in his tone. "What's the word, Lord? Was that you back there?"

"Hell yeah, it was me. Some niggas just tried to slide through the alley on us in a burgundy Oldsmobile. Think it might've been a Delta 88. They was masked up, and one of them had a Mac. I fired the whole car up."

Seeing that there were no police in sight, he inserted a fresh, thirty-round mag, made a U-turn in the middle of traffic, and began to search for the Oldsmobile as he headed back in the direction it had fled. When he passed Christiana, he saw that Pig, Big Keanan, and three more TVL gang members were loading into Pig's big, white Suburban.

"We just saw you ride past," Big Keanan said.

"Yeah, I'm looking for that burgundy Delt right now," Lil Luke replied. "If y'all see it first, flip that bitch."

Chapter 10

Voltaire made half a dozen phone calls to his younger brother, Keondre, and their Zoe Pound boys back in Miami, and within minutes, he had twelve men packing their bags to board a private jet that would land in Chicago three hours from now. Since the flight was privately owned and their bags weren't likely to be searched, the twelve Haitians were bringing a trove of weaponry along with them. Rugers and Glocks and Sig-Sauers, Dracos, and AR-style pistols and sawed-off shotguns. The works.

During the phone calls, Voltaire stood, leaning back against the closed bathroom door, and kept a watchful eye on Eva. She'd given him directions to her Aunt Candace's house, a fairly spacious, single-family residence at the far end of Nahas Drive, just off US Highway 20. It had huge Rottweilers chained to the dog houses in the equally massive backyard. There was an old, rust-laden, dark blue, 1980s model Chevy Caprice parked just inside the fence. Voltaire had parked the box truck right beside it.

Pocketing his phone, he looked over at Eva. She was sitting on the closed lid of the toilet, texting her twin sister on her iPhone, her hands trembling furiously as she did it. Voltaire tried wrapping his mind around the fact that she was only seventeen and failed miserably. She looked twenty-seven. Her juicy, pink lips beckoned him. Her fat, round ass spread out nicely on the toilet lid. She had a gorgeous brown face with sexy wisps of baby hair matted down along the front of her hairline. Her brows were done. So were her fingernails. And she smelled like Heaven.

"Why are you shaking?" Voltaire asked, using an elbow to thrust himself off the door. In two short steps, he was in front of the toilet, standing over Eva. "There's nothing to worry about. You'll be just fine. We'll get your mother back."

She looked up at him, her eyes slowly narrowing to stringent slits. "Why am I shaking? Is that what you just asked me? You just shot up that truck like it was nothing! Like you was in some kinda action movie! The fuck?! That's why I'm shaking."

Voltaire chuckled once. "Come," he said and opened the bathroom door.

He went out to the living room where he'd left his black, leather Fendi duffle bag next to a coffee table that resembled an oversized Rubik's Cube with a circular slab of glass laid over it. He sat down on the colorfully upholstered sofa and looked up to find Eva sauntering toward him in her skintight jeans and snow-white iKiss hoodie, her small, delicate hands buried in the front pocket.

"Ganja?" Voltaire inquired as he dug in his duffle and lifted out a Ziploc bag containing close to eight ounces of high-grade marijuana.

"I need to get to my truck." Eva stood next to the sofa and looked at the widescreen television she'd turned on when they first walked in. A Dojo Cat video was playing, though with the vacant gaze Eva was giving it, you'd think the TV was still turned off.

"We'll get to your truck soon enough," Voltaire replied.

He took out a packet of organic blunt wraps and tore one open. He started rolling himself a blunt while he pondered over what he would do to Markio the next time he crossed paths with the bumbaclot.

There would be blood spilled for certain. Large pools of it. And there would be fingers and toes and ears in that dark crimson puddle. Severed lengths of flesh and bone that belonged to Markio Earl.

When he looked up and saw that Eva was still staring blankly at the television, he took her by the elbow and pulled her down onto his lap. She resisted but only for a second. Then, she sighed and turned to face him.

"You know what, Voltaire? I can't even blame you for getting me into that situation. I shouldn't have gotten in that box truck with you from the start. That was karma, and that bitch bit me right in my ass."

"No, no, no. No karma." Voltaire closed an arm around her waist and kissed her on the jaw. "Everything happens for a reason. It's all part of God's plan. We just go with the flow."

He fired up his blunt and used one strong, black hand to maneuver Eva's legs so that she was facing him with her knees planted on either side of him.

The position made for an enticing view.

For a few minutes, the two of them passed the blunt back and forth, occasionally flicking rolls of ash into an ashtray on the end table next to them. The living room's décor was all LGBTQ+ with plenty of photos of Candace and her sexy, dark skinned girlfriend, Tika, hanging from the walls and standing in wooden picture frames on the tables. They were the kind of lesbians Voltaire loved to see, the kind where both women were feminine and beautiful and eager to show their love for each other through public displays of affection, but right now, Voltaire's gradually narrowing eyes were focused exclusively on Eva.

He imagined life with Eva without her mother in the picture and decided it might not be so bad. Giving financial support to a boss bitch like Whitney required hundreds of thousands of dollars, and supporting Eva would undoubtedly be a lot less expensive. He'd seen Whitney's financial statements. She'd been wiring each of her four children about $2,500 every couple of weeks. That was nothing compared to the quarter million he'd blown on a Birkin bag, a diamond Rolex, and a few high-end designer outfits for Whitney just last week.

"Reach back there and pick up my duffel," Voltaire said, rubbing his hands back and forth along Eva's meaty thighs as she sat toking on the remaining half of the blunt. "Just something for ya."

He noted the crease at the side of her mouth as she turned to do it, an incipient smirk. She strained to lift the heavy duffle bag.

"Shit. The hell you got in here?'

Voltaire reached forward and took hold of the straps. He set the large cylindrical bag down next to them and undid the zipper. He spread it open to allow Eva a look inside.

There was a lot going on inside the duffle bag — $180,000 in brand new hundreds, all bundled into the ten thousand dollar packets he'd gotten from his bank in Miami Beach, Florida, the AR pistol he'd used to shoot up the flashy, blue Volkswagen truck that belonged to one of Markio's boys, three additional fifty round banana clips, his gold handled machete, a change of clothes, and two bricks of cocaine he and his gang had taken from Markio's stash house.

"Know any dope boys out this way?" Voltaire asked Eva as he picked out a packet of hundreds and slipped it into the belly pocket of her hoodie.

"Psshh. I know all the dope boys. They're all in my DMs. I got trap niggas from here to California on my pussy, and I ain't fucked none of them."

Voltaire nodded and lifted out a kilo of coke. He placed it and his AR pistol next to him on the sofa and then zipped the bag shut and dropped it back onto the floor while Eva took the packet of hundred dollar bills out of her pocket and utilized one impeccably manicured thumbnail to fan through one corner of it.

A glorious smile spread across the width of her incredibly gorgeous face. She giggled unexpectedly. She wiggled her ass on Voltaire's lap and threw her head back and screamed with excitement.

Voltaire laughed out loud. "Settle down," he said and planted a quick kiss on the side of her neck. "Get on your phone and make some calls. See if you can find somebody to buy this coke. We've got money to make."

Chapter 11

"You've got some serious explaining to do," Alexus said in a frigid, venomous tone.

Markio eyed the stunningly attractive drug cartel queenpin's ice cold expression as she stared back at him on the screen of his iPhone. He'd made it to Michigan City. His Cullinan was parked in front of the Comb Street house where Whitney's three daughters lived. Ava and Joselyn had come out onto the front porch and were standing there with their arms folded across their chests, waiting on Markio to exit the truck.

Meanwhile, judging from the palm trees swaying about in Alexus Costilla-King's background, she was soaking up the Florida sunshine from the comfort of her sprawling Miami Beach mansion. Bojo, her overly muscled personal bodyguard, stood over her right shoulder, glowering into the camera.

"I'm taking care of it," Markio said to Alexus. "I figured out who set it up. It was my ex, the bitch who started the iKiss company. She was mad at me over some money she felt like I owed her, so she sent her boyfriend, Voltaire, at my stash house."

"Voltaire?" A wrinkle appeared between Alexus' eyebrows. "The guy who runs the Zoe Pound?"

Nodding his head, Markio glanced over and saw that Jarvon's gaze was unwaveringly fixed on Whitney's beautiful teen daughters.

"That's what I hear," Markio said, speaking to Alexus but watching Jarvon. "I don't know the nigga or nothin', but I heard he got it for the Zoes. All I know for sure is that his brother, Keondre, is the highest paid running back in the NFL. I don't really watch that shit, but I looked it up this morning."

Alexus went silent on him, a silence that lasted a long while. "So," she asked finally as Markio's red-veined eyes returned to her deadly green ones, "where is this Whitney? Where can I find her?"

Markio hesitated. Then, "In Chicago. Fo'nem got her tied up. I just called and talked to one of them. He say they had just fucked her up and was about to go ahead and kill her, but I told them to hold off on all that. Don't get me wrong, she done set me up to be robbed twice — the first time she had some young niggas break in my house, and the second time was this whole shit with Voltaire, but I don't wish death on her." He clenched his teeth. "I'ma kill that nigga, Voltaire, though. On King Neal."

Alexus' eyes lit up very suddenly. "Hey, that's my son's name," she said, beaming. "Text me the location to wherever they're holding this Whitney chick. I want to see her for myself."

Markio studied the sinister smile on the multibillionaire's sexy, brown face. There was an underlying evil to it that made him hesitant to reveal the location where Whitney was being held. Sure, Whitney had wronged him, but he didn't want anything bad to happen to her. His only reason for having her kidnapped was to get her to tell his boys where they could find Voltaire. After that, as far as he was concerned, she could be set free.

"Don't hurt her," he said after a thoughtful pause.

"She'll be fine. I just want to talk with her. Text me the address."

Alexus ended the video call, and Markio gave Apple the nod to get out and open his door, which was what the chubby man did. Jarvon pushed open his own door and got out with his hand on the Glock under his shirt, looking around.

When Markio stepped out of the Cullinan, his eyes immediately fell on the line of young Black men and women who were filing a house at the end of the street. Jarvon looked that way too. Markio knew that the men were Gangster Disciples, most of them from Gary, Indiana. The name of their clique was the Joka Mobb. Their leader was a dark, pudgy man called Pimp. He looked a lot like Miami rap icon Trick Daddy, and he was at the front of the pack, leading the way toward two snow-drizzled SUVs that were parked at the curb.

Two of the boys threw up the rakes, a pitchfork-like hand sign consisting of the thumb and forefinger pointed up at the sky with the middle finger sticking up between them. It was the Gangster Disciples hand sign. Markio gritted his teeth at the sight of it and reached inside his jacket for his own Glock pistol, but the two rogue gangbangers looked away, as did their leader, and the bunch of them began piling into the SUVs.

"What's poppin', five?" Jarvon asked, his Glock in hand now, his long, brown fingers closed tight around its handle.

"Let 'em go," Markio said, shifting his attention back to Ava and Joselyn as he entered their front yard through the gate of their newly installed wrought iron fence.

The two girls were shivering in the cold winter weather, their every breath accompanied by a cloud of smoky vapor. Joselyn had tears in her eyes, but they didn't fall down her pretty, round face until Markio was ascending the porch steps toward her.

"Please tell me you know where my mama at," Joselyn implored as she fell against Markio's chest and hugged him. "Tell me something. We haven't heard anything."

"Come on. Let's go inside. It's cold out here," Markio replied.

It was a diversion, meant to offer himself a moment to contemplate an answer that didn't sound like bullshit. Kids were smart these days. You couldn't just get away with telling them any old thing.

Ava gave him a small hug when they entered the doorway. There had always been a no shoes on the carpet policy in Whitney's home, but it seemed the kids had done away with it in her absence. The usually spotless pink floor rugs were stained in places, and the house had a different smell to it.

No one went to the sofas. Ava stood before Markio with her arms folded across her chest, Joselyn with her hands on her hips, both of them regarding him with silent anticipation.

He was just opening his mouth to speak when he heard a dull thump from somewhere overhead. He tilted his head back and looked up at the ceiling.

"That ain't nobody but Jimmy," Joselyn said quickly.

Lil Jimmy was Whitney's oldest child. He was also her only boy. Last Markio had heard, Lil Jimmy was living in an apartment with his girlfriend, Crystal.

The swiftness with which Joselyn had spoken sounded a bit off to Markio, but he thought nothing of it.

"I talked to a few of my niggas in Holy City," he said. "That's where we was at when they snatched her outta that parking lot. Don't nobody know who did it yet, but everybody's saying they saw that Avalanche circling the block for about an hour before the kidnapping. It didn't actually pull in and park until around the time that nigga, Trell, got stomped out in the restroom, so I'm guessing somebody in the strip club must've texted or called the kidnappers, letting them know the club was about to get shut down. I think whoever took her might be waiting for shit to die down, so they can contact somebody and demand a ransom. Whatever it is, I'll pay it, and we'll get her back."

"I'm saying though," Joselyn said, "that's your hood, right? That's where you came up. You know those people. Why can't you just…"

"Whoever took her wasn't from my neighborhood," Markio lied. "I'm on it. I promise." He looked around the room, knowing that Eva wasn't present but acting as if it surprised him. "Where y'all crazy ass sister at?"

"I told you already," Ava said in a near whisper. "She left with Voltaire."

"Where did they go?"

Ava shrugged her shoulders and averted her gaze. "I don't know," she said in an even lower tone. "She stopped answering my texts."

Markio was no fool. He was a reader of body language. Ava knew where Eva and Voltaire had gone off to. She just didn't want to tell him.

He looked up at the ceiling again. His expression hardened. Markio had a ton of love for Whitney and her children, but the fact remained that there were millions of dollars' worth of narcotics involved, pounds of exotic bud, and kilograms of cocaine, heroin, and fentanyl that had been delivered to him on consignment from northern Mexico's reigning drug cartel. He couldn't just let that go, no matter the toll it might take on his relationship with the Clarrett family.

He looked back at Jarvon and Apple. He gave them a nod and motioned his head toward the ceiling. That was all it took for Jarvon to draw his pistol, and two seconds later, Apple had his out as well.

"Go upstairs and see if that's Voltaire," Markio ordered, and he quickly turned back to the girls to gauge their reactions.

Joselyn's glossy lips fell apart. Ava's eyes widened, and an audible gasp escaped her throat. She raised both hands in front of her, palm out, fingers splayed. It was a pleading gesture.

"No!" Ava said. "It's only Jimmy! I swear!"

"Good," Markio said. "Then you shouldn't mid if they go up there and check. They know what Voltaire looks like."

"She's lying," Joselyn muttered, staring down at the toe-end of one Jordan sneaker. "It's Flocka and his cousin, Benji. Her boyfriend and my boyfriend. She didn't want you seeing them for some reason."

Ava had nothing to say to that. Two seconds later, Apple barked for someone to get up and walk downstairs with their hands in the air. There was a brief shuffling sound, as though someone fell forward, and then a flurry of thudding footfalls as Jarvon and Apple led the two boys back down the stairs.

Markio took out his own Glock pistol and leveled his gelid gaze on the two teenage boys as they entered the living room with their hands held high above their heads. They were both dark in complexion, though Flocka was a shade or two darker that Benji. They both wore designer joggers and Nike Air Max sneakers. Markio knew them well. Flocka had hung around the house with Lil Jimmy back when Markio and Whitney were together, and Benji was a close friend of Markio's nephew, Tyquan.

But there was only one thing that came to Markio's mind when he and Flocka locked eyes. Flocka was one of the two young thugs Whitney had sent to break into Markio's house. Markio had suspected Whitney of cheating on him with the brawny young dreadhead until now. There was no way Ava would be dating him if he'd been with Whitney first.

Flocka looked fearful. His eyes moved from left to right again. From Markio to Jarvon. From Jarvon to Apple, who'd pulled the red ski mask back down over his face, from Apple to the gun in Apple's hand, because the gun was pointed at him.

Jarvon went in Flocka's pockets. He snatched out a bankroll, an iPhone, a wallet, a set of keys on an Adidas keyring, and a baggie full of Xanax pills. He threw the keys to the floor, pocketed the other items, and then checked Flocka's waistline for a pistol. Finding none, he went to Benji and searched him just as aggressively. Benji's bankroll was even thicker, and he had a gold Rolex watch on one wrist. Jarvon hastily relieved him of those belongings.

"Oh, my God, Markio," Ava said, cupping her hands over her mouth. "Please. Stop."

Markio shook his head no. "Nah, fuck all that. These hoe ass niggas know what it is. I should whack these fuck niggas right here."

Jarvon swiveled his head to stare questioningly at his older cousin, roughly pressing the barrel of his pistol against Flocka's left temple.

"How you wanna do it, five?" Jarvon asked in his peculiar Louisiana dialect. "You already know what it is wit me. We put guns to the face. Who gon die today?"

Ava's eyes grew even wider as she swung her head to stare at Jarvon. Joselyn reacted in similar fashion, as if Jarvon's distinctive voice was one they recognized from somewhere. Benji even turned to look at him.

"I honestly don't know where Eva and Voltaire went," Ava said, still staring at Jarvon. "I swear to God. She left out with Voltaire about an hour ago, and she texted me saying not to tell you who she was with. I can show you the messages."

She did just that, walking over to the coffee table to grab her phone with tears undulating along her lower eyelids, her hands shaking tremulously as she went to the text thread and showed it to Markio.

"Sis, pls don't tell Markio who I'm wit. Volt just shot up Blubby's truck! IDK what's going on but it's crazy! I'll call u in a few. Tryna figure out what happened to Mama."

Markio nodded his head and turned to look at Flocka's glowering face. He'd become an enemy to Markio through no fault of his own. Whitney was a wicked woman when she wanted to be. She'd reeled Flocka in — likely through one form of seduction or another — and he'd fallen for the bait — hook, line, and sinker.

"Y'all niggas sit down on that couch over there," Markio said, motioning with his pistol. "Ava, I'ma need you to call your sister and get that location for me. Voltaire got something that belongs to me, and I need that back."

Ava stood there, staring at Markio, with tears trickling down her comely, reddish-brown face. She was blinking, saying nothing. She glanced at her boyfriend and his suave-looking cousin as the two teen boys moved past her with their hands still raised above their heads and dropped down onto the sofa.

With an overly dramatic roll of her eyes and an audible suck of her teeth, Joselyn un-pocketed her own iPhone and said, "I'll call her now."

The living room was dead still as Joselyn dialed her big sister, Eva's phone number and let everyone listen to the ringing on speakerphone. Markio's mind seemed to race to a different thought with every ring of the phone. He thought of Whitney's condition after Chubb and Rev had "fucked that bitch around," as Rev had told him on the phone. He looked at Flocka and Benji and remembered the night they'd helped his nephew, Tyquan, fend off a home invasion in a shootout that had ended with Tyquan being shot in the stomach and two of the attempted burglars shot dead. He thought of Voltaire and tried to guess where he and Eva might be. A motel? One of Eva's friend's apartments?

When the call went to voicemail, Benji said, "Man, can we put our arms down? My shit hurting like a bitch."

Markio gave them a reluctant nod, and they lowered their hands to their knees. Jarvon became extra vigilant as they did it, aiming his Glock at them and moving closer.

"Does this have anything to do with what happened to our mama?" Ava asked, wiping the tears from her face.

Before Markio could offer up another lie, Joselyn said, "You really shouldn't even be out here, Kio. You know my friend, Dejane, is cool with the chief of police. He said they believe you're behind ninety percent of the unsolved murders in this city. He thinks you're the one who shot G-Money in the head and that you paid Shannon and Sway to kill those two boys who used to be with him over there on Cedar Street."

Markio had no response to either accusation. He turned to Jarvon. "Give 'em their shit back," he said and dug in his pants pocket to grab his rubber-banded bundle of cash. He slipped out a ten-thousand-dollar packet of hundreds and tossed it to Flocka two seconds before Jarvon dumped their belongings onto the coffee table.

"Put us on, big bro," Benji said. "We ain't on no bullshit with you. That whole shit with Flocka and Mellie Mel breaking in your house was because of Whitney. She paid them to do that shit. We been rocking with your nephew ever since we first moved up here from Evansville. Flocka would've never done that shit if Whitney hadn't..."

"Wait a minute." Ava cut in. She planted her hands on the hips of her skintight jeans and shifted her attention to her boyfriend. "Wait one fucking minute. What does he mean Whitney had you and Mellie Mel break in Markio's house? Why am I just now hearing of this?"

Flocka waved her off. "I ain't about to talk about that shit with you right now," he said. "That's between me and your mama." He looked at Markio. "All I can say is I'm sorry, my nigga. Shit, my right-hand man got killed right there on your back porch when we did that shit, and I almost got shot up right there with him. She was supposed to give me fifty racks for breakin in to steal eight suitcases, but they wasn't there, so she only gave me five bands."

"Well," Markio said, holstering his pistol, "that's ten bands I just gave you for helping my nephew that night. And I got another quarter million for you if y'all can find that nigga, Voltaire, for me."

Flocka and Benji turned to each other with wide eyes, but Markio didn't see it. He had already turned to leave. Jarvon walked backwards with his pistol still aimed at the two boys until he, Apple, and Markio were at the front door, and he kept his gun in hand as they made a beeline for the Cullinan, Apple rolling his mask up to his forehead, Markio casting a furtive glance across Michigan Boulevard at the sprawling hilltop building that housed the Michigan City Police Department.

His phone rang as soon as he sank down into the butter soft leather of his backseat. It was Lil Luke.

"Lord, some niggas just tried to slide on us," Lil Luke said. "Pig recognized the car. It was the Breeds from off Thirteenth and Sawyer."

"Y'all ain't air 'em out?" Markio asked, thinking of the twenty-three Austrian-made Glock switches he'd donated to the gang.

"Bruh, you know I aired 'em out. I emptied the whole thirty and got outta there. They sped off too, and by the time we caught back up with 'em, they had flagged down the police on Albany."

"Y'all know who it was?"

"Nope," said Lil Luke. "But we did find out who Steel is. He one of the Breeds off Thirteenth. Big ol' ugly nigga who just got out the joint. You might remember his sister, that big booty bitch who used to fuck with Big Sam. Lord n'em whacked her son some years back. Guess Steel hot about the shit. His other nephew's girlfriend was driving, so I know it was him who sent 'em. I shot the shit outta one of them niggas."

Lil Luke began to laugh, but Markio didn't find anything funny. He remained stone-faced, picking up his Styrofoam from the cup holder and taking a generous sip. Apple started the engine while Jarvon tucked his Glock away and brought out the Draco.

"Slide down Sawyer and drop some'n," Markio said to Lil Luke. "I should be back in town sometime tonight. I got a bag on Steel's head too. Fuck it. I see I'ma have to start showin' these niggas what all this money can do."

Chapter 12

Neetra was on her knees, pounding the carpet with her bare fists and howling out the soul gripping sounds of a hurting Black woman. Skip stood next to her, running the palm of one hand up and down her back, whispering consoling words in her ear.

Bent forward with his thick, brown fingers displacing the blinds over their living room picture window, Steel stood tensely with Skip's Mac 12 in one hand, his smooth, bald head glistening with perspiration despite the frigid winter temperatures. Skip moved to the sofa and struggled to keep his hands off Tammy, the redbone thotty who was standing next to him.

An hour had passed since Steel's nephew, Pojo, was shot six times in the chest and shoulder while riding in the backseat of his girlfriend's car. He was holding on. According to one doctor they'd spoken with at Northwestern Memorial Hospital, he had a fighting chance of surviving. His girlfriend, Elise, had taken a round through the elbow and another two through the shoulder. Skip had made it through the shooting without so much as a graze wound.

"Ay, lil mama," Steel said to Tammy, "go back there and grab me that last beer out the 'frigerator." Tammy nodded her head and sauntered off toward the kitchen, her shoulders raised as if expecting an ice-cold wind to blow through the room.

The heat wasn't working. Neetra's landlord was supposed to be sending someone to fix it. Steel had gone out and purchased five space heaters from Walmart, but the place was still a little chilly. Tammy wore a plush red Fendi trench coat, while Steel sported black Nike sweatpants with a matching hoodie and black Timberland boots. He had a bunch of cash in his pockets. He'd withdrawn seven thousand dollars from his bank account — two grand for himself and five for his nephews — but they failed to kill anyone, so he'd only given Skip a thousand dollars. He knew that Tammy's only reason for stopping by was to extract some semen from Skip's dick in exchange for three or four of those crisp new hundreds.

Steel wasn't thinking about anything but revenge. His eyes were on the red, brick house directly across the street from Neetra's building. A pregnant girl named Alycia Duncan lived there, and word on the street was she'd been impregnated by Big Keanan, an outstanding member of the Dark Side TVLs from 15th Street. There was a blacked-out Dodge Challenger parked at the curb in front of Alycia's place. Skip said it was Big Keanan's car, so Steel was watching it like a hawk.

"They shot my baby!" Neetra sobbed, rolling over onto her hip to stare pleadingly at her older brother. "Them punk ass niggas done shot my Pojo! I want 'em dead, Steel! I want every last one of 'em dead!"

She was an emotional wreck. Skip went to his knees beside her and wrapped his arms firmly around her shoulders. He kissed her on the side of her forehead and spoke a steady flow of consoling whispers.

"Don't even worry about it, lil sis," Steel said. He had yet to move from the window. "We gon get our lick back. I can promise you that. If a nigga don't die about this shit, my name ain't Steel Toe."

His name wasn't Steel Toe. No one had ever called him that. He'd tried to make the nickname stick several times over the years, because he liked the sound of it, but everyone had stuck with Steel.

"That shit wouldn't have happened if Skip wouldn't have froze up when it was time to blow," Steel said. In his peripheral, he saw Skip's eyes flick over in his direction, and he nodded in response to the glowering stare. "Yeah, nigga, you heard me right. How in the hell did you manage to let a nigga pop out on y'all and shoot up the whole car when you had this big ass Mac 12 in yo hand? You was supposed to shoot the fuck out that boy."

"That boy had a Glock with a switch!" Skip said snappishly. "Do you know what the fuck that means? Have you seen a Glock with a fuckin switch? Huh? Here, let me show you."

Skip was on his feet in an instant, leaving his mother to grieve on the floor, while he whipped out his smartphone and searched "Glock switch" on YouTube. He found the video he was looking for and thrust the phone at Steel.

"Here you go. Look at this shit and then tell me if you would've been able to shoot back."

Steel took the phone and watched the thirty second video. It showed Fredo Santana, deceased member of Chief Keef's Glory Boyz empire, firing two Glocks at the same time. Fire and smoke belched from the barrels of both pistols as they sprayed fully automatic gunfire at a paper target in the distance. The fifty round drum magazines were depleted in just three or four seconds.

A hundred rounds fired in mere seconds.

"Mm hmm," Skip hummed, reacting to his uncle's stunned expression. "Ain't no shootin back when a nigga run down on you with somen' like that. All you can do is duck and pray."

Tammy returned from the kitchen with Steel's beer. He cracked it open and took two replenishing gulps. "You're right, nephew," he said a few seconds later. "Niggas didn't have that kind of fire power when I left the streets twenty-one years ago. Damn."

"The whole Dark Side gang got switches on their Glocks," Tammy said. "That's how they killed Esco across the street from my old apartment on Douglas and Albany. Shot him like thirty times in the head. Killed his boys too."

Gritting his teeth, Steel turned back to the window and fingered the blinds down. He raised his lower lip over his upper lip and flared his fat, black nostrils. He nodded his head again. Neetra rose to her feet and staggered into her bedroom and collapsed onto her bed. Steel only saw it out of the corner of his eye. He was focused on the street out front, sweeping his gaze from one end of the block to the other. Tammy's blood-red Tahoe was parked right behind his white Nissan Rogue, and he wondered what she did for a living to afford such a nice vehicle. It had big, red rims on it and darkly tinted windows, and it looked brand new.

Steel was considering turning around to speak with Tammy when the front door to Alycia Duncan's house swung open. He motioned for Skip to join him at the window, and the two of them watched as a thuggishly dressed, young, Black man in his early twenties stepped out onto Alycia's front porch. The man looked back into the house and shouted something then laughed and let the storm door slam shut behind him as he started off down the steps.

"That's Travis," Skip said, "Big Keanan's lil brother."

Steel didn't say a thing. He simply handed Skip the Mac 12 and went back to staring out the window as Skip put his ski mask on and snatched open the front door.

Tammy gasped from somewhere behind Steel, and Neetra must have sensed the palpable tension because she appeared in her bedroom doorway, wide eyed and wet faced.

"Tammy," Steel said quickly, "go out there and start up your truck. Give him a ride to the airport right after he drop this nigga. I'll meet you there with Neetra. I got a few hundred for you."

"Okay," Tammy said just as quickly, and in an instant, she was out the door, hurrying down the hallway stairwell behind Skip, and shouting for him to slow down.

Neetra rushed over to the sofa and kneeled on the cushion to peer out the blinds like an excited kid looking for the neighborhood ice cream truck. Only there was no excitement in Neetra's eyes. She was hurting. Her pink, Fendi bathrobe went up over her hips, exposing her fat, round ass and the string of her pink, lace, Savage X Fenty thong. Steel was tempted to sneak a glance at her enticing, meaty backside, but he was much more interested in what Skip was about to go do in front of the building.

The block was far from vacant. Karo, Meatball, and Hank, three lifelong New Breeds who were much younger than Steel and much older than Skip, had just pulled up in a blue minivan two houses down from Alycia's place; they were climbing out of the minivan when Skip came running out the front entrance of the apartment building. Pinky — a fat redbone who lived next door to Alycia — and her four children were lifting plastic bags of groceries from the trunk of her Kia sedan and carrying them into her house. Three other young, Black women were passing blunts around inside a blue Ford Explorer a little farther down the block while a Sexyy Red song blared from the speakers. One of them lowered her window to shout out at Travis just as Skip was crossing the sidewalk on Neetra's side of the street.

"Heyyy, Travis! With yo lil fine ass!"

Travis looked her way and smiled, but only for a second or two. That smile swiftly morphed into a frown when he caught sight of the masked young man darting toward him from across the street.

Instinctively, Travis reached under his black leather Pelle Pelle jacket and closed his hand around the butt of a pistol just as Skip raised the Mac 12 and opened fire.

PHOP! PHOP! PHOP! PHOP! PHOP!

Ducking his head, Travis drew his pistol and tried to take aim, even as several bullets burned holes through the chest of his jacket. Pinky screamed and threw two bags of groceries to the ground as she grabbed her two young sons and took cover beside her car. Travis fell backwards, squeezing off a series of gunshots as he went down. His pistol fired like the guns Steel had watched in the YouTube video. The rounds punched a dozen holes across the side of an unoccupied Chevy pickup truck that Skip had just crouched beside to fire over the hood, and Travis seemed to give in to the pain, looking up to the sky as he kicked and flailed on the walkway in Alycia's front yard, clawing at his wounded chest, his eyes and mouth stretched wide with panic.

Skip ran around the front of the pickup and sprinted into Alycia's yard to stand over the dying young man. He shot Travis four or five times in the face, and Travis stopped flailing.

Beside Steel, Neetra gasped and covered her own gaping mouth with both hands, but Steel kept his eyes on his nephew as Skip scooped up Travis' pistol, ran back across the street, and jumped in the passenger's seat of Tammy's shiny new Tahoe. Tammy had already gotten in behind the wheel. She started the engine and raced off down Sawyer Avenue, leaving behind one dead man and numerous traumatized eyewitnesses.

Steel had Meatball's phone number. He'd gotten it from Meatball's uncle, Pumpkin, a feminine, gay man he'd let suck his dick a time or three when they were housed together at Menard Correctional Center. He took out his phone and dialed the number, watching the Explorer as it peeled off in reverse.

Meatball and his boys had crouched low beside the minivan, two of them drawing their own pistols. They rose slowly now, looking around, repeatedly glancing at the unmoving body in Alycia's front yard. Pinky left her spilled canned goods scattered on the sidewalk as she hurriedly ushered her children into their house. Two older, Black men came walking up the sidewalk on Neetra's side of the street, their hands resting on their hips as they stared across the avenue at Travis' lifeless corpse. They looked like dope fiends.

The phone line was ringing in Steel's ear when Meatball produced a smartphone from his pants pocket and looked at it. He ignored the call; Steel gritted his teeth and called back.

"Can't talk right now, OG," Meatball answered.

"Just make sure them bitches in that Explorer don't say shit about what just happened."

"We got it." Meatball shot a glance at Neetra's living room window. Then, he turned to the two old men across the street from him and shouted, "Aye, y'all ain't see shit!"

Both men raised their hands in surrender, and before Steel ended the call, be heard them shout back that they hadn't seen a thing. Meatball and Hank slipped their pistols back into their waistlines. They climbed back into the minivan and pulled off at a normal speed, making a U-turn in the middle of the street and driving off in the direction the Explorer had gone.

Steel connected his phone to the charger and stepped back from the window with a triumphant smirk playing at the corner of his mouth. He smacked Neetra on the ass, and she spun around on the sofa, rubbing her stinging buttock with one hand and wiping the tears from her face with the other.

"Ouch," she said, dropping her damp Kleenex tissue into her bathrobe's side pocket. She didn't look anywhere near as upset as she had before the shooting. "I can't believe he just ran up on that boy and shot him like that. I ain't know he had that in him."

"Call Pinky and make sure she keeps her mouth shut," Steel said. "And get dressed. We got a flight to catch."

Chapter 13

Long, yellow ribbons of crime scene tape blocked off 13th and Sawyer from both ends of the block, and there were CPD vehicles everywhere when Lil Luke and Jaybo rode past in Lil Luke's triple black Dodge Charger Hellcat. Someone had draped a white sheet over the body in Alycia Duncan's front yard. The evidence markers that stood next to every spent shell casing looked like miniature yellow pyramids with black numbers on them, and there was a trail of them that led from one side of the street to the other.

"Goddamn," Jaybo said, shaking his head. "That's Travis."

"I know, man." Lil Luke couldn't believe it. "That lil nigga wasn't even in the streets. Keanan sold that brick of fentanyl to Juice and sent Travis over here to drop a few bands off to Alycia."

They could see Big Keanan standing there behind the yellow tape with his mother, his three younger sisters, and about twenty other family members, all of them sobbing and hugging each other as they grieved the loss of Travis McCall, the twenty-three-year-old who was perhaps their family's greatest hope at escaping the trenches.

Lil Luke had known Travis personally. While Big Keanan squandered his days and nights hustling in dope houses and gang banging with the TVLs, Travis had started purchasing foreclosed properties, renovating them, and selling them for a profit. He was engaged to a stunningly attractive realtor from Buffalo, New York. He owned a brand new 2023

Cadillac XT6, but he had an affinity for muscle cars, so he'd opted to drive Big Keanan's Challenger Hellcat to Alycia Duncan's place. Alycia was Keanan's longtime girlfriend and mother of his two young sons. She was eight months pregnant with her and Keanan's first daughter, and Travis had already bought the baby everything she'd need. He'd been a doting uncle to all of his nieces and nephews and a comedically entertaining presence to the rest of his family and friends, so much that Lil Luke wondered who the loss would affect more, the kids or the adults.

A white, female police officer standing with four other cops at the corner of 13th and Sawyer turned and gave Lil Luke's car a long, hard look as he cruised past. Her interest in them was understandable; they were two young, Black men with lengthy dreadlocks and tattoos on their faces, sitting in a fast car with tinted windows, passing through one of the most crime ridden areas in North Lawndale. Lil Luke was surprised she didn't jump in one of the squad cars to try chasing them down.

He looked away from her and drove on, feeling nervous all of a sudden. He had his Glock under his right thigh. Jaybo's was on his hip. Lil Luke also had a bottle of ten milligram Percocets and over three thousand dollars cash stuffed down in one pocket of his Amiri jeans. If twelve got behind them, he was going to the dash.

He made a couple of turns, sped down some alleyways, got back on 16th Street, and rode past Christiana to look down the alley behind Pig's house. There was a cop car parked there. Either someone had called the police and reported the sounds of gunfire, or the Chicago Police Department's "Shot Spotter" had pointed them in the right direction. Whatever the case, Lil Luke wouldn't be posting up on the block for a while.

He phoned Markio and let the call play on the Charger's sound system.

"What's the word, big homie? You heard about Big Keanan's lil brother?"

"Nah, what happened?" Markio asked.

"Shit, a nigga just whacked him. Keanan sent him over there to his baby mama's crib on 13th and Sawyer to drop off some bread, and one of the Breeds ran out the building across the street and blew him down with a Mac. Hit him all in the face. Pinky called my daddy and told him it was some lil nigga named Skip. She recognized him by his shoes."

"Thick ass Pinky who used to live on Central Park?"

"Yup. Tweet Body's baby mama. She fat as hell now. Said she was taking some groceries in the house when the shit went down."

"Make sure she don't say shit to twelve."

"Man, you know she ain't gon say shit to them people. She said make sure nobody shoot up her house on accident."

Markio went silent for a long moment as Lil Luke whipped into the vacant lot on the side of 1530 South Trumbull Avenue and pulled up next to his cousin Sheisty Lord's burnt orange 1996 Chevy Impala SS on thirty-inch rims. He and Sheisty were renting from Rell and Tamera, one of the most successful Black couples he knew. Rell and Tamera, along with Rell's younger brother, Jah, and Tamera's older sister, Tirzah, owned more properties in the North Lawndale neighborhood than anyone else in the whole community, and they'd come up in the very same trenches. Rell had changed for the better. He wore suits and ties now, drove a shiny black G-Wagon, gave back to the community with turkeys for the less fortunate on Thanksgiving and gifts for school-aged children on Christmas. Jah, on the other hand, was still neck deep in the streets. He drove a blacked-out Lamborghini that was rumored to be bulletproof. He sold kilos of cocaine and heroin to all the trap millionaires, and he was deeply involved with the gang wars that were currently raging all over the west side of Chicago.

There was another vehicle parked in the vacant lot, a dark blue Explorer. He and Sheisty Lord lived on the first floor of the building. An older man called Long Game lived with his wife on the second floor. The basement apartment wasn't rented out, but it was furnished, and recently, Jah had started using it to sneakily link up with other bitches behind his wife Tirzah's back.

"Damn," Markio said finally. "I thought I told y'all to go over there and drop some'n. How did they end up droppin one of us?"

"We hadn't even made it over there yet. I rode past there once and didn't see nobody. Then, Keanan started saying he wanted to catch them niggas somewhere else 'cause his baby mama stay right there."

Markio sighed. 'I'm out here in Indiana tryna find this nigga, Voltaire."

"And you ain't take no security with you?" Lil Luke asked incredulously.

"I'm good. I got Apple and my lil cousin, Slime, with me. We got two Dracos and four Glizzies in this Cullinan. I'll flip some'n in this bitch."

Shaking his head and looking over to watch the GloRilla video Jaybo was looking at, Lil Luke said, "Bruh, don't do that shit again. You got the bag, nigga. We can't be taking them kinda risks. Oh, and it was that nigga Steel's nephew who shot Travis. Big Booty Neetra's son. That's who Skip is."

"Hm." Markio went silent. Then, "I got a fifty on that lil nigga Skip."

"Fifty?!"

Lil Luke and Jaybo said it simultaneously, their eyes bulging out of their heads.

"Yup. Fifty thousand. Catch him and stretch him. I'll call you back."

Markio ended the call, and for several seconds, Lil Luke and Jaybo just sat there, staring at each other in disbelief.

Jaybo was the first to break the silence. "Elise! She fuck with his brother. I know we can pay her broke ass to set the pick."

"I shot that bitch earlier today," Lil Luke said. He'd seen it on Facebook. Someone had shared Elise's post, a video of her in the hospital with her arm all bandaged up and cradled in a sling. She'd informed everyone that Pojo was in surgery, that he'd been shot six times, and that the doctors were saying he had a good chance of surviving.

He and Jaybo tucked their pistols and pushed open their doors. They exchanged ideas on how to catch up with Skip as they crossed the frozen lot and ascended the concrete porch steps, both of them remaining watchful the entire time. They were accustomed to urban warfare. Lil Luke had shot up one of the Breeds, and that Breed's brother had retaliated by shooting Travis dead. There would likely be three or four more shootings in the next twenty-four hours. Lil Luke wasn't trying to get caught lacking and neither was Jaybo.

Not that they had anything to worry about on 15th and Trumbull. The block was as dead as Travis McCall. They had both heard stories about the days when Trumbull was the place to be, but nowadays, most of the action went down on Christiana (or "the Ana," as everyone called it). Christiana was where the younger members of the gang hung out. No opp would even think of looking for a victim on Trumbull Avenue.

But Lil Luke kept his hand on the butt of his Glock anyway. Just in case.

He was approaching the porch door when someone on the opposite side of it turned the knob and pulled it open, and suddenly, he found himself staring into the mesmerizing green eyes of Noesha Long.

She gasped and brought a hand up to her chest, and then, her pretty mouth formed an enticing little smile. Two of her friends were with her — Quita, a brown skinned beauty with an ass that was even fatter and rounder than Noesha's and

Lacey, a six-foot two-inch Amazon who bore a striking resemblance to LSU basketball star Angel Reese.

When the moment of stunned surprise passed, Lil Luke smiled and chuckled and stepped inside. The porch door opened into a well-kept hallway with a staircase on the right that led upstairs to the second floor apartment.

"What the hell y'all doing over this way?" Lil Luke asked as he looked Noesha up and down.

She wore a fluffy, yellow, Moncler jacket over skintight, black sweatpants and black and yellow Jordan sneakers. Her long mane of hair was colored golden blond and parted straight up the middle. Her fingernails and eyebrows were expertly done, and as she regarded Lil Luke with a sexy open-mouthed smile, he could see a flattened wad of chewing gum stuck to the lowered teeth on one side of her mouth.

She smelled good enough to eat.

"Hmmm," she said. "I should be asking you the same thing. My daddy lives upstairs. I just came over to bring him some cigarettes. I think the real question is why you are stalking me like this. I mean, damn, liking all my pics is one thing, but you can't be following me around and shit."

Quita and Lacey laughed out loud. So did Jaybo, who added, "Yeah, you might be right on this one. He definitely been stalkin yo page."

"Whatever, shorty." Lil Luke breezed past her. "I live right here." He went to his front door and slipped in his key, unable to erase the amused smile from his face, and the image of Noesha wiggling her fat, yellow butt cheeks in a colorful pair of booty shorts flashed across his mind. He looked back over his shoulder as he pushed open his door and was pleased to find her staring at him with a portion of her succulent lower lip pulled in between her teeth.

Lacey dug a folded pile of cash out of her own bubble Moncler jacket — hers was white with Moncler embroidered across the back in black and gold lettering. "Fuck all that.

Who got the zah?" She asked the question as she thumbed through the bills. There were only a few denominations in her bankroll. Tens and fives for the most part.

"I got that same loud pack Pig got," Lil Luke said, taking a weed filled baggie out of his jacket's inside pocket and dropping it on his coffee table as he plopped down on the black, leather sectional in his living room.

He was using the half ounce of high-grade marijuana like a worm on the end of a fishing hook, and the three bad bitches chomped right down on it. He placed his Glock on his lap as they filed into the living room, Noesha staring at him, Quita and Lacey looking around the room and nodding their heads in agreement with its lavish décor.

Lil Luke had grown up poor, but those days were long gone. His father was Luke Duke, the Dark Side TVL who'd left the streets in his rearview to start his own record label, the music producer who'd introduced the world to a number of Chicago rap artists, including Grindo, the drill rapper whose debut album had gone on to sell more than three million copies worldwide. Luke Duke's girlfriend, Pandy, was best friends with a real-life billionaire, and the two of them had been spoiling him ever since he lost his mother when she was shoved off a train platform a few years ago. They'd taken good care of him while he was in prison, and they'd gifted him the Charger and $30,000 cash when he got his case overturned and came home.

He'd spent most of the money on clothes and furniture. The sectional alone had cost him $6,500. Pandy had bought him the eighty-inch smart TV that stood along one living room wall. She'd also paid for the black twenty-six-inch Forgiato rims that had his Dodge Charger Hellcat sitting up like a monster truck, and it seemed like every other day he received another package she'd purchased for him from Gucci, Prada, or Dior.

Once all the girls were inside, Jaybo pushed the door shut and locked it. Quita looked back at him with suspicion in her lashy brown eyes.

"Y'all ain't slick," Quita said, rolling her eyes and twisting her neck.

"For real though," Lacey added. "He done locked us in this bitch."

"Hell yeah." Lil Luke nodded his head, his unwavering gaze fixed on Noesha. He patted the seat next to him and scooted over a bit. "You can sit right here next to me."

"We can't stay for long," Noesha said as she took the seat beside him and set her yellow Chanel handbag on the table. "Nya will throw a whole fit if we're not waiting in that parking lot when she gets off work."

Lil Luke was shaking his head, shaking his dreads. Noesha looked over at him and rolled her eyes laughingly. Lacey produced a pack of Backwoods cigarillos from another jacket pocket. She and Jaybo began rolling blunts. Lil Luke asked if anyone wanted to drink, and when all the girls nodded yes, he got up and disappeared into the kitchen, returning seconds later with a chilled bottle of Hennessy and a stack of red plastic Solo cups.

"We just saw some crazy ass shit over there on Sawyer," Quita muttered as Lil Luke set four cups on the table and started pouring an equal amount of cognac into each cup. "Some nigga ran down on Travis and killed him right in front of us. I mean, we saw the whole thing. We actually just watched him die in somebody's front yard."

Jaybo and Lil Luke both swung their eyes in Quita's direction. She was the only one still standing, and she had her sexy, brown face angled downward, seemingly staring at the toe-ends of her Ugg boots. Her phone rang silently in one hand. Lil Luke glanced at the phone screen and read the contact name.

Hank Daddy.

"You ain't gon' answer that?" Jaybo asked.

Quita shook her head no. "They've been calling us ever since that boy killed Travis," she said, raising her head to look at Jaybo, her eyes replete with worry. "I don't want nothin to do with them boys over there. Lacey's the one who hooked me up with Hank anyway 'cause she was fuckin' with Meatball's lil dirty ass."

"Shit," Lacey said, really stretching out the word. "That boy got some gunfire head. He ate my pussy so good the other night that I fell off the washing machine and broke three fingernails."

"Wait a minute," Jaybo said. "So, y'all was there when Travis got killed?"

"Mm hmm," Noesha answered. "The boy had a mask on. A ski mask. He jumped in a red Tahoe after he did it, and the slim, lil redbone bitch he had with him sped off."

"But I thought they said he ran out the building and started shooting?" Lil Luke asked.

"He did. And that slim, lil redbone was with him. He ran out the building and started shooting, and she ran out the building and got in that Tahoe. She was a pretty girl too. Had on a long, red, Fendi coat. I know it was Fendi 'cause I saw the Fs all over it. He jumped in the truck with her, and they jetted off."

The girls started talking about how they had sped off in reverse, but Lil Luke and Jaybo didn't have anything else to say on the matter. They locked eyes with each other and then went back to doing their thing, Jaybo rolling a second blunt, Lil Luke slipping an arm behind Noesha and turning to examine her up close.

Lacey's phone was ringing like Quita's. They had both put their ringers on silent, but Lil Luke saw the screens lighting up incessantly. They would look to see who the caller was and then look away.

Lil Luke drank from his cup of cognac when Noesha drank from hers.

"What's it gon' take for me to get you in that bedroom back there?" he asked when his attraction to Noesha became too overwhelming to bear.

She sucked her teeth and gave him a stale side eye. "Boy, I got bills to pay. My sister, Niecy, just had a baby, and I ain't bought the lil girl nothin' 'cause I ain't even got my own shit together."

"I got a lil bread for you."

"You ain't got enough."

"What's enough?"

Noesha hesitated. She had an iPhone in her hand, one of the larger models. She was on Instagram, and every couple of seconds, she'd swipe her thumb up the screen to peruse another photo or video. The people she followed were mostly professional athletes, movie stars, and rap artists. Lil Luke saw Ja Morant, Lil Baby, Anthony Davis, and Nicki Minaj.

She want a nigga with some money, Lil Luke thought to himself. *Somebody who can afford to have her dressing like those celebrities.*

His thoughts dissipated as he watched Noesha leave Instagram for YouTube. She searched *Bills, Bills, Bills* and pressed play on the Destiny's Child song. She skipped to the part where Bey sang about the need of a man who could pay her bills then maybe later they could chill. Lil Luke laughed when she raised the volume and replayed it.

He had to wrestle the fat pile of cash from his pocket, and out of the corner of his eye, he watched Noesha light up with excitement. He had a red rubber band wrapped around the cash, and all the Benjamins were on top. There were seven hundred-dollar bills, eight fifties, and ninety-seven twenties.

"Yeah!" Lacey said, her eyes widening at the sight of the thick pile of cash. "Now you talking, lil Daddy. Bring them racks out."

"Y'all know who his pops is?" Jaybo asked the girls, and when the three of them turned to look at him, he said, "Luke

Duke. The Grammy-nominated music producer. The CEO of Dark Side Records."

Noesha and her two friends became even more excited.

"Okay," Noesha said, nodding her head and slipping her phone back into her handbag. "We might be able to work somethin' out."

Chapter 14

Whitney Clarrett had grown numb from the searing hot pain in her gut and was spiraling in and out of consciousness when she heard a booming shout that inspired an inkling of hope.

"Chicago Police Department! Everybody on the ground! Now!"

The shout was followed by several jarring sounds, the first being a rattling of steel against concrete, the second being a violent explosion that was accompanied by a blinding flash of light and a burgeoning cloud of thick, gray smoke. Then, a cacophony of frightening sounds merged to become one great chaotic noise — a hard mechanical pop hitting the floor then another.

Forcing open one brutally swollen eye, Whitney tried lifting her head to figure out what all the commotion was about, half expecting her captors to be playing some cruel joke on her in which they pretended to be saviors in uniform, here to protect and serve, when really they were merely setting the stage for another inhumanly barbaric torture session. But she saw no such thing. What she found standing all around her were black military-style boots and camouflage pants. (Raising her head high enough to see anything above the waist was literally impossible.)

There was blood on the floor under her chair. Her blood. The sight of it made her vision fade out again but not before a snow-white pair of stiletto heels appeared in between all the boots. The feet wedged inside them were cute, light brown in complexion, and expertly pedicured. The lower part of a full-length, white, fur coat hung elegantly around her ankles, and the wearer of the fur was holding a gold plated 7.62-millimeter Draco pistol down by her right side. The largest diamond ring Whitney had ever seen in her life twinkled on the ring finger of the woman's left hand.

Whitney had seen the ring before. She'd seen it quite a few times in fact. On TMZ, and Instagram, and Good Morning America, and CNN. It belonged to Alexus Costilla, the gorgeous Black and Mexican woman who'd recently overtaken Elon Musk to become the world's wealthiest person, the woman whose entire paternal family had been indicted and ultimately acquitted for allegedly leading the most ruthless drug cartel in all of Mexico, the two hundred billion dollar woman who owned the Minority Television Network, The Costilla Hotel and Resort in Cancun, five Costilla oil refineries, and MTN Studios, among hundreds of other businesses, the A-list celebrity whose Instagram following of more than four hundred million people made her the most followed woman on the platform.

The woman who'd recently posted a photo to Instagram that showed her posing inside her Miami Beach mansion with Markio Earl was standing right beside her.

Shit, Whitney thought, and then, she lost consciousness.

Chapter 15

Belly was, and always had been, one of Voltaire's all-time favorite movies, not only because of the Jamaican culture, but also because the things depicted in the film were so closely ingrained with his own Haitian culture, and also because of the films all around impact on Black culture as a whole.

Right now, he felt like Tommy Buns, the character DMX had played in the iconic film, only instead of a sixteen-year-old bad bitch sucking him off in a convertible, he had a seventeen-year-old bad bitch sucking him off in a hardtop sedan.

The car was a 2023 Mercedes Benz S580. He'd just rented it from Dub Life Autos on US Highway 20 for a mere $244.81 per day, and he'd gotten it for seven days. He and Eva were riding down Willard Avenue, her soft, pink lips gliding up and down the length of his hard, black dick while he sat back in the heated leather driver's seat and spoke on the phone with Scarlette "Lady Zoe" Toussaint, a forty-year-old female Zoe Pound member who'd been putting in work for the gang for over two and a half decades.

The time was 4:44 p.m., and Lady Zoe had already arrived, packed the stolen kilos into twenty-nine cheap, black, duffle bags, and loaded the duffles into the three triple black, presidential ESV Escalades she and the other Zoes had driven from Chicago's Midway Airport to Candace's place in Michigan City, Indiana. The motorcade of Cadillac

SUVs were already back on Interstate 94, en route back to the airport.

"Are you sure you'll be able to make the flight?" Voltaire asked Lady Zoe as he steered the luxury sedan past a church across from Bee Kay's, the convenience store, at the corner of 9th and Willard.

There was a collection of tricked out vehicles parked alongside the store — two 1970s model Chevy Caprices on gold, thirty-inch rims, a white Chevy Suburban on chrome, thirty-inch rims, and a light blue Buick Park Avenue on chrome and white, twenty-eight-inch floaters. Most of the occupants were inside the vehicles, and the two men who weren't were clearly dope boys. They wore Amiri and Givenchy joggers, designer jackets, and diamond jewelry.

"One hundred percent," Lady Zoe assured him. "We just did it last week. Sent a hundred and twenty pounds of meth to Junie in Kansas City. They won't even think of searching our plane. They'd have no probable cause."

Voltaire nodded his head as if Lady Zoe could see him as he spun the steering wheel to make the turn onto 9th Street. He parked next to the curb just across the street from the store and reclined his seat a little. Eva was giving him a slow, sensual blow job. She was nowhere near as orally skilled as her mother, but she was good enough. She knew to keep her mouth nice and wet and to apply a certain amount of suction as she rode his dick with her tongue and lips. Every ten or twenty seconds, she'd go down a little too far. She'd gag and cough and lift her head from his lap to stroke his saliva coated dick in both hands until she caught her breath, and then, her warm mouth would return to sucking him, and he'd inhale deeply at the glorious feel of it.

He had just taken her shopping at the Lighthouse Mall. The trunk of his rented Mercedes was filled to capacity with shopping bags from Lids, Gap, Timberland, Victoria's Secret, Vanity Fair, Shoe Carnival, Tommy Hilfiger, Rolex, and Nike. He'd blown close to thirty grand of his own cash on her, and she'd also spent a few thousand out of her $10,000 pockets of hundreds, mainly because she'd bought clothes and shoes for her sisters as well.

Confident that Lady Zoe and the others would be able to load the stolen kilos onto his brother, Keondre's private jet without detection, Voltaire ended the phone call and sat back with a smile on his face. He eyed his reflection in the rearview mirror and studied the twinkling diamonds on his teeth. He wore jewelry like the boys on the corner, only his was worth a lot more than theirs.

Looking beyond his own reflection, he stared at the grimy, young, Haitian man who was slouched down in the backseat behind him. The boy was called Shotta Zoe by all who knew him. He was nineteen-years-old, dark skinned, and beady eyed with an incipient mustache and five thick dreadlocks that hung down around his head and reached past his shoulders. The AR-15 rifle he held across his lap had a two hundred twenty round drum magazine attached to its underside and a green laser beam mounted under the long, black barrel. The boy was dressed in Celine from head to toe, and his teeth blinged with diamonds just like Voltaire's.

"Me lady friend here tells me this is where the ex-boy used to hang out," Voltaire said to Shotta Zoe's reflection. He closed one hand around the nape of Eva's neck and gave it a gentle squeeze. "Isn't that right, sweet thing?"

Eva nodded her head with her slippery lips wrapped firmly around the enormous girth of Voltaire's dick. She'd undone her YSL belt and pushed down her jeans and thong panties and was now kneeling on the passenger's seat with her head bobbing in Voltaire's lap and one hand wedged between her thighs, fiddling with her clitoris one minute, penetrating herself with two fingers the next. She'd lowered the volume on the R&B playlist she'd put together more than an hour ago, and the Muni Long song playing now was hardly even audible. Voltaire massaged Eva's impossibly soft derriere in one hand, wincing once as her teeth grazed the head of his throbbing hard erection.

"We should've just left with the bros," Shotta Zoe commented. "Let him come and find us in Miami. On our turf. We'd destroy him there, but what do we know of this place? Hmm? We're at a disadvantage. These are his people."

Voltaire shook his head in disagreement. "He's from Chicago. He may have met these people, but he doesn't know them. And knowing is half the battle."

"He knows more about them than we do," Shotta Zoe muttered discontentedly.

Voltaire dismissed the spicy responses. His eyelids fluttered, his bare ass tightened against the smooth leather of his seat, and he inhaled a quick breath as he spurted several geysers of slimy, white goo into Eva's steadily sucking mouth.

She froze with her lips sealed firmly around the gushing head of his dick. Her gorgeous face took on the expression of someone whose mouth had suddenly been filled with the vilest sauce ever created. Voltaire held onto the nape of her neck to keep her from taking her mouth off his convulsing organ, clenching his teeth as the semen shot out of him.

"Swallow it," he said shakily. "It's good for you. The protein."

He smiled when he heard the first hard gulp. Then came a second noisy gulp and a third and finally, she raised her head, squeezing the last few drops of cum out of him and licking the globs off the tip of his fat, black snake of a penis.

Voltaire shivered twice and chuckled once. Eva was still wearing the disgusted face, though with a face as flawlessly beautiful as hers, it was impossible for her to show an expression that Voltaire didn't find sexy. He pulled up his expensive pants and put away his deflating member. He buckled his high-end designer belt, picked up his half smoked blunt from the ashtray, and put fire to the end of it.

"Yuck," Eva said as she pulled up her own designer jeans and wiped her mouth with the palm of her hand. She reached for the twenty-ounce bottle of Sprite she'd purchased when they stopped at the gas station, and Voltaire watched her contracting throat muscles as she drank a good eight ounces of the cool beverage in two long gulps. "That was the nastiest shit I've ever swallowed in my life."

With another amused chuckle, Voltaire turned his head to look at the boys across the street. A few of them were watching the Benz. They couldn't see through the tinted windows but they clearly wanted to; one of them, a short, brown-hued, stocky young man in a brown leather Gucci letterman jacket over denim jeans and tan Timberland boots, had his head lowered and was swaying from side to side like a charmed King Cobra snake as he attempted to get a glimpse of whoever was driving the Mercedes.

Voltaire put the car in drive and glided off slowly, toking on his blunt as Eva began texting on her phone. Every couple of seconds, she'd make a hacking noise as she attempted to clear the last vestiges of semen from the back of her throat.

"That was AJ trying to look in the car back there," she said. "Markio fucks with him heavy. They say Markio was the one who gave him all that weed. My friend, Dejane, said he sold thirty pounds to some scammer in Cleveland two days ago. He paid her some bands to drive that load out there. He got a cute ass baby mama too. Shaquilla Walker. Bitch got more ass than me and Ava put together."

"AJ, huh?" Voltaire nodded, stroking his goatee as he made a left turn and drove past a gated brown building with no markings on it. It looked like a group home of some sort.

He kept going and made another left onto 8th Street. He was circling around, heading back toward the store, only instead of taking Willard Avenue this time, he crossed it and continued on to Grant Avenue where he made a left turn and accelerated up to the alleyway that led out onto Willard right beside the church — right across from the convenience store.

He slowed down as he turned into the gravel alleyway. Up ahead, he could see the rear ends of two 1970's model Caprices. AJ and another guy were standing just outside the store's glass side door. A sign that read JoJo's Chicken hung above the door. Rambling along down the alley, Voltaire watched a heavyset, Black man exit the glass door holding a Styrofoam food tray in one hand and a lidded Styrofoam cup in the other.

He pointed at the fat guy, and Eva said, "They call him Cookie. He buys weight from Markio and sells it to the younger dope boys out here. I heard he was the one BD Raw was coppin his dope from until they got into it at Shay Cooper's club in Gary."

Eva had just introduced Voltaire to BD Raw — a tall, rail-thin Renegade Gangster Disciple with gold teeth and dark skin — in the Lighthouse Mall parking lot about twenty minutes ago. She'd sold BD Raw a kilo of cocaine for $40,000 cash. BD Raw had the money in a brown paper bag with Al's Supermarket printed on both sides, and after tasting the dope, he'd driven off in a brown, candy-painted 1970's model Buick Electra 225 on gold thirty-inch Forgiato rims.

Voltaire pumped the brake and pulled over behind the redbrick church building, the tread on his tires crunching through two or three inches of snow. He passed the blunt over his shoulder to Shotta Zoe. He shifted into park and let the car idle with the heat blowing for a fleeting moment then reversed and turned the car around to face away from the convenience store.

"Be honest with me," Eva said, twisting in her seat to look straight at Voltaire. "Is Markio behind my mama's disappearance?"

Voltaire didn't hesitate. "Absolutely. He owed her over two million dollars and was refusing to pay, so I robbed his stash house. He was mad about that, so he had his gang kidnap your mom."

He glimpsed a flare of evil flash across Eva's usually angelic visage. She picked up her phone and went to a video she had saved to her photo gallery. It showed Markio giving her a hug next to a table at one of his book signings.

"That bitch ass nigga," she muttered in wavering tones of incredulity.

Voltaire snapped his fingers to get Shotta Zoe's attention and adjusted his rearview mirror to lock eyes with the trigger-happy young killer. "Run over to that store and kill the boy in the brown jacket. You kill him, I pay you good, and you go home a lot richer than you came."

A blast of cold air rushed into the car when Shotta Zoe pushed open his door. Eva turned to stare at Voltaire. Then, she spun in her seat to look out the darkly tinted rear window as Shotta Zoe went running out of the alleyway onto Willard Avenue.

When Voltaire's gaze returned to his rearview mirror, Shotta Zoe was just raising the AR-15 and taking aim at someone across the street.

Thunderous claps of gunfire ensued.

Chapter 16

Markio was on the phone with Big Keanan, delivering his condolences and informing him that he just sent $50,000 to Keanan's mother, Sharae's bank account through Zelle, when three jarring gunshots caused him to flinch as the sixteen-year-old memory of the day he himself was shot on the front porch of the very same house he was now standing in surfaced before his mind's eye.

He recovered quickly, ended the call without a proper goodbye, and drew his Glock from his Louis Vuitton shoulder holster. He looked at Jarvon "J-Slime" Barnett with wide, alert eyes and then crossed the living room to the front door in three long strides.

They had been gathered in the living room of Samantha Tucket's house. The mint green clapboard home was just across from Bee Kay's convenience store. Markio had directed Apple down the side streets, and he'd had the fat guy park his Rolls Royce Cullinan in the alleyway behind the single-family home. Samantha and her sexy, yellow bone friend, Tayja Walker, were pouring drinks at the kitchen table when the gunshots rang out; they too flinched, and Tayja reached for her purse to retrieve her own Glock pistol.

They'd come to Samantha's house for a reason. Markio had fronted Tayja ten bricks of cocaine almost three weeks ago, and she'd messaged him this morning saying she had $240,000 for him. He'd only charged her $280,000 which meant that after this pickup, she'd only owe him another forty grand.

The cash was stacked across the brown living room carpet and on the ancient wooden coffee table in rubber band bundles. Each bundle had a piece of paper stuck beneath the rubber band that displayed the exact amount of cash the bundle held. Slime had just snapped open a Glad trash bag to begin filling it with cash when they heard the first three gunshots.

Slime had purchased a green Gucci bandana earlier in the day. He had it tied around his neck with the knot at the back, and he pulled it up to cover the lower half of his face as he dropped the trash bag and snatched the mini-Draco from inside his joggers. Markio threw open the door and stepped out onto the front porch with his Glock raised and his eyes squinted against the frigid breeze. Slime appeared beside him a second later, but he hardly noticed it because. in the next fleeting moment, he witnessed his old friend, AJ, get skewered by several rifle rounds to the back as he and another nigga named Fonzo attempted to run around the side of the store that faced 9th Street. Their 1973 Chevy Caprice Donks were parked along the Willard Avenue side of the store — the side where the gunfire was coming from.

Critically wounded, AJ fell to one knee on the slush-coated sidewalk, and then, he went down on his belly. Markio's eyes swept the block from left to right, searching for a shooter, but he didn't find one. The gunman was obviously standing somewhere near the mouth of the Willard Avenue alleyway, which was out of Markio's eyesight, obstructed by the three-story, redbrick church building.

Several people pushed open their car doors and jumped out, ducking for cover beside their vehicles. Fonzo reached back around the side of the store building and fired blindly, squeezing off multiple shots from a large, black handgun.

There was movement in Markio's peripheral, and when he flicked his eyes that way, he saw a black Mercedes sedan go speeding backward through the alleyway next to the church. It was headed in the direction of the unseen gunman.

That's Voltaire, Markio thought, but then, he reminded himself that Voltaire was driving a white box truck, not a black S-Class Mercedes.

Markio and Slime both leaped off the concrete porch and crossed the walkway in Samantha's front yard with their firearms raised. They ran up the middle of 9th Street. It took them less than ten seconds to get to Willard, and when they did, Markio looked to his left and immediately spotted the gunman. The dark-skinned boy with fat dreadlocks hanging down around his head and an AR-15 assault rifle cradled in both hands was firing round after devastating round at Fonzo, high caliber rounds that knocked dusty chunks from the gray, stone storefront.

The gunman turned his head and spotted Markio and Slime standing half a block away from him with their guns in hand. He swung the barrel of his rifle in their direction, but Markio already had his fully automatic Glock raised. He let off ten or twelve shots before the dread head could let off a single one. Slime opened up with his mini-Draco. The boy rocked from side to side as his frail, young body absorbed the bullets like in the movies. He fell away into the alley, and Markio and Slime took off down the sidewalk, chasing after him.

Markio was fast on his feet, but Slime's legs were longer; therefore, his strides were longer, and he made it to the mouth of the alleyway two whole seconds before Markio did.

What they saw when they got there stopped them in their tracks.

Voltaire was standing outside the open driver's door of the Mercedes with one big forearm wrapped around the front of Eva Clarrett's neck. He was holding an AR pistol to the side of her head. The dreadhead gunman was crawling toward Voltaire with blood pouring from his wounded torso, using only his knees and his one good hand to scurry forward. The assault rifle lay half buried in snow against the side of the church.

"You kill him," Voltaire threatened, "I kill her. It is as simple as that."

Slime had his mini-Draco pointed at the back of the gunman's head, while Markio's modified Glock was trained on Voltaire's forehead. Looking at him now, Markio could see how Whitney had fallen for him. Voltaire was a big, muscular man — tall, dark, and handsome, the kind of man women lusted over,-and he wore diamond Cuban-link necklaces and an icy wristwatch just like Markio.

"I have your kilos," Voltaire said, easing his head behind Eva's to keep Markio from getting a clear shot. "And you have my woman. When you release her, I might consider a negotiation. That is it."

"You know you're dead, right?" Markio said, his forefinger wrapped firmly around his Glock's double trigger.

Voltaire cracked a devilish smirk. "Step back right now or I kill her. I give you three seconds. One…"

Almost unconsciously, Markio took two steps back.

Slime didn't budge. He kept his mini-Draco trained on the wounded gunman, staring the boy down as he staggered forward and fell against the driver's side of the Mercedes, dripping blood into the fresh layer of snow.

"Your friend there is going to get this little one murdered, and her blood will be on your hands," Voltaire said.

"Slime, come on," Markio said. "We'll catch this hoe ass nigga later."

A dark, ominous laughter erupted from the bowels of Voltaire's rock-hard abdomen as he watched Markio and Slime step back around to the front of the church. Behind them, people were screaming that AJ and a girl named Crystal had been shot. Police sirens sounded in the distance.

"See you in Miami," Voltaire barked a moment later. Markio heard several car doors slamming shut. Next came the distinctive churning of pebbles in the gravel alleyway as the Mercedes went speeding off. Markio peered around the side of the church just in time to see the Benz's brake lights flash red as it fishtailed out from the opposite end of the alley and vanished from sight.

As he and Slime turned and ran back toward Samantha's house, Markio glanced across the street at AJ's fallen figure. He was gasping for breath, his arms and legs flailing restlessly about. Fonzo was crouched over him, yelling for someone to call for an ambulance. A few sets of eyes turned to watch the two richly dressed young men run back into the fenceless front yard of Samantha's dilapidated single-family home. All of them knew Markio personally, and he was almost certain that neither of them would say a word to the responding police officers.

But he still needed to hit the road and fast.

Samantha, a curvaceous, half white, half Puerto Rican mother of six, was standing in the living room with her hands on her hips. Tayja stood next to her with her subcompact Glock in one hand and her phone in the other, breaking the news of AJ being shot to her cousin, Shaquilla, the mother of AJ's two young sons.

Without a word, Markio and Slime began scooping up bundles of cash and dumping them into the trash bag. Samantha started helping just as Apple came waddling through the front door with a dollop of chocolate glued to the corner of his mouth.

"Man, y'all hear all them gunshots?" Apple asked, sucking his fingers and balling a plastic cupcake wrapper in one fat fist. "Somebody just got shot at the corner store over there."

"Nigga," Markio said, slowly and coldly, "if you don't get cho big, hungry ass down here and help me pick up this money, you gon' be the next motherfucker to get shot."

The threat elicited a humorless chuckle from the corpulent man, but he quickly pocketed the cupcake wrapper and got down on his knees to help load the cash into the garbage bag.

Markio's phones were ringing nonstop. The police sirens were growing louder. When he glanced up and caught sight of Tayja standing there in her tight, blue sweatpants, his gaze lingered on the jutting curves of her hips. She, too, was of mixed race — half white, half black — and she had just as many children as Samantha, but her body was so tight and sexy that it seemed she had birthed no children at all. She wore gold rings on most of her fingers. Her hair was partially braided to the back on one side and styled in a neat shoulder length bob on the other. The blue hoodie she wore had a photo of her deceased brother, Tristan, printed on the front.

She showed a small grin when she saw that Markio was staring at her, and he hastily shifted his attention back to the cash piles. *Stay focused*, he told himself. Tayja was one of his biggest crushes. In prison, he'd often fantasized about dicking her down, and he'd told all his guys that he was going to marry her when he touched down. Unfortunately, God had made other plans, and he'd ended up with Nikkia, and unlike Tayja, Nikkia wasn't in the streets.

Switching gears, Markio thought of Voltaire and clenched his teeth menacingly. A part of him regretted not shooting Voltaire when he had the chance, but that was only his selfish, angry side. At the end of the day, he had morals and values to abide by, unspoken human laws that took precedence over any gang literature he'd ever learned, and those ideals had taken the reigns in the life-or-death situation. He possessed a special kind of love for Whitney and her family, a love that wouldn't change, no matter how much she angered him. He couldn't risk accidentally shooting Eva, and he definitely hadn't wanted Voltaire to kill her. That memory would have haunted him for eternity.

An ambulance and two Michigan City Police Department vehicles arrived at Bee Kay's. Samantha had pushed the front door shut, but the venetian blinds over her picture window were open, allowing for a perfect view of the corner store. When they were finished loading the cash into the trash bag, Slime yanked the string on the bag to shut it, and Apple used the corner of the coffee table to lift himself to his feet. The three men went to the blinds, and before the six policemen investigating the shooting could look their way, Markio grabbed the rotating stick attached to the blinds and spun it until the blinds were shut. Heart racing, he turned to the motley group standing before him.

One of the policemen standing at the corner was former chief Martin Switztek. Swizz, as he was called, had been relieved of his duties and demoted to the rank of police lieutenant after Michigan City experienced a string of unsolved homicides under his leadership. Campbell, a Black, former MCPD detective, had taken Swizz's throne.

Markio Earl was the leading suspect in the unsolved homicides.

"We can go out the back door," Markio said. "We'll have to make a U-turn in the backyard and leave the alley from Grant Avenue. Hit Willard on 10th and ride past the prison heading south."

"Man, I don't know what none of that mean," said Apple.

Markio took out his phone and typed the directions into Google Maps before sharing it with Apple. He peeked through the blinds one last time — the cops were speaking with eyewitnesses and rolling out yellow tape, while the medics loaded AJ into the ambulance on a stretcher — and then lowered his head, pulled his designer skullcap down over his ears, and made a beeline for the back door. Slime and Apple trailed him outside and through the unshoveled backyard. His ankles were already cold from the snow he'd encountered in Samantha's front yard, and now, they became even colder.

"Wait!" Tayja shouted, and when Markio looked back, he saw that she was jumping through the snow behind him, moving hurriedly to prevent her fur-lined designer boots from becoming too dampened. "I came with AJ. He was my ride over here."

Markio was halfway tempted to tell her to hail an Uber, but there was no way he could ever say such a thing to Tayja Walker, and it wasn't just because he liked her. Tayja was the type of gangsta bitch who might try going upside his head if he denied her a ride, especially after she'd just handed him close to a quarter of a million dollars. And besides, Markio liked the idea of sharing an intimate moment with her in the backseat of his Rolls Royce truck. He'd have time to speak with her in private to tell her some things he'd been wanting to say for more than two decades.

She got in beside him, while Slime joined Apple up front. Even with all the adrenaline coursing through his body, Markio couldn't help but to smirk as he watched Tayja settle into the seat.

"We shouldn't have let them niggas live, five," Slime complained from the front passenger's seat. "Voltaire could've died today, ya heard me? Could've died right there in that alley. Him and his lil guy."

Markio said nothing. He took out his two iPhones and read the text messages he'd received from Chubb, and Lil Luke, and Shannon Swanson. Chubb told him that a group of men claiming to be CPD officers had burst into the house they'd had Whitney confined in. The phony cops had tased him and Rev and escaped with Whitney. Lil Luke said he was at home with some bad bitch named Noesha. He'd sent a video of the girl sitting his living room sofa, and it made Markio look over at Tayja as she rubbed her hands together to warm them.

The text message from Shannon Swanson was the one that really got Markio's attention. "Bro, that nigga, Voltaire Muck, just rented a Benz S580 from Stephanie. It's all black with tinted windows and factory rims. He had one of Whitney's daughters with him when they pulled up at the car lot. Got a GPS on the car, just let me know if you need it."

Stephanie Swanson was Shannon's gorgeous older sister, a dark hued woman who was approaching fifty but looked half her age. She and her two brothers, Swayson and Shannon, were the owners of Dub Life Autos, a luxury car dealership they'd founded just a few months ago using the cash Markio had paid the Swanson brothers to drop a few bodies for him.

Markio's spirits rose, and he smiled expansively as he texted back. "SEND ME THAT GPS ASAP!"

"What the hell got you so geeked up?' Tayja asked, smiling as she dug a pack of Newports out of her Chanel purse. "And can I smoke in here?"

"It ain't shit." Markio picked up his Styrofoam cup from the cup holder and drank from it. The ice cubes had melted, but the Wockhardt syrup and Sprite beverage was still relatively cold. "Yeah, go ahead and light up. I don't care. You can do whatever you wanna do back here."

"I'm trying to quit." Tayja lit the cigarette. "Shit, I can't help smoking this one. My cousin baby daddy just got shot up right there on the corner. I can't believe that shit,"

Markio only looked at her. Her brother, Tristan, had been one of his best friends, one of the first guys he'd met when him, his mother, and his siblings first migrated there from Chicago more than twenty years ago, and he'd always told Tristan how much he liked Tayja. She was the epitome of a dime piece with a mulatto complexion and a body like the mouthwateringly thick R&B songstress Queen Naija. She was a Gangster Disciple, like the rest of her family, but none of that mattered to Markio. He didn't socialize with many GDs in Chicago, but here in Indiana — namely in Michigan City, Gary, East Chicago, Hammond, Anderson, Evansville, Fort Wayne, South Bend, and Indianapolis — he knew droves of them, and most of them had a lot of love for him. Like Tayja, they knew he was a real nigga, the kind of man you could trust to never fold under pressure, the kind of man who'd never betrayed a friend and likely never would, and

105

perhaps most importantly, the kind of man who would never hesitate to shoot his pistol when he and his loved ones were in danger.

"We shot the nigga who hit AJ up," he said to Tayja. "He got away, but I know we both shot him. Them Draco shells probably fucked him up. He might not live."

Tayja inhaled deeply, exhaled, and picked a couple specks of lint from the thighs of her Moschino sweatpants. She smelled like Chanel's latest feminine fragrance; Markio had recently purchased the same perfume for Nikkia.

"I did what Big Meech did with the bricks he was copping when he ran BMF," she said in her misleadingly soft voice. "Took an eighth out of each brick and replaced it with cut, and I sold them for forty racks apiece. Still got five and a quarter brick left. One of my baby daddies was about to buy those, but I ended up making a better deal with a white boy named Ray Ray from Elkhart. He offered me forty-two thousand apiece for the other five keys, so I'm waiting on him for my profit."

Markio calculated the money she'd made selling the first six kilos and realized she'd given him every dollar of it. He tugged the fat stack of hundreds out of his right-hand pants pocket, snapped off the rubber band, and began thumbing through the enormous pile of crisp new Benjamins.

"You gave me everything you made?" Markio asked, giving Tayja another glance.

She nodded. "Yeah, but it's cool. I wanted to get you out the way first. I got another two hundred thousand on the way that I'm keeping for myself, and I'ma give the money I make off that last quarter brick to Samantha. I plan on taking care of my kids and starting me a clothing line with the money I make on the back end."

Markio shook his head. "Nah, I'ma put you up somewhere nice. I'll give you the money you need to start that clothing line. You can just spend your money on clothes and whatever else you and your kids need."

He placed two ten-thousand-dollar packets of cash on her luscious left thigh. As he did it, the tip of his pinky finger brushed gently against the blue cotton fabric, and the flesh beneath it felt so incredibly soft that he instantly become aroused, his dick lengthening and hardening in his Versace boxer briefs.

"You don't have to do this," Tayja said as a tear formed in her eye. "I don't mind working for my money. You already did me a huge favor fronting me those ten bricks. I'll be straight for a long time off that."

"You just did me an even bigger favor. You made me a quarter million dollars richer. That was the ultimate favor."

Apple turned around in the alley and followed the directions Markio had given him, and soon, they were rolling away from the growing police presence at the corner of 9th and Willard. Markio was on his phones the entire time. He revealed to Chubb that the so called CPD officers who'd burst into his basement were actually Mexican drug cartel members. He told Lil Luke to enjoy himself with the bad young yellowbone. He received the GPS history of Voltaire's S-Class Mercedes and smiled when he saw that the Benz had driven from the scene of the shooting straight to St. Anthony's Hospital. From there, it had gone to Southgate Apartments, a sprawling apartment complex on the city's south side.

Coincidentally, the directions Markio had given Apple took them down a nearly deserted back road that led right past Southgate Apartments.

Markio reached over the back of his seat and into the spacious rear storage area. He shoved the big trash bag full of cash aside and lifted one of his duffle bags back over the seat. He took out the mini-Draco and rested it across his lap.

Tayja gave the Draco pistol a double take then tucked the stacks of hundreds into her purse and brought out her own pistol.

"I take it you're going after the man who shot my cousin's baby daddy," she said.

"Yup." Markio smiled. "And I know just where to find him."

Looking straight ahead, he gave Apple directions to the southside apartment complex and watched as an MCPD sport utility vehicle went screaming past them, likely racing toward the crime scene they'd just fled. He could see Tayja studying his gaudy appearance out of the corner of his eye. Her studious gaze sent a warm flood of pure bliss splashing through his chest cavity. He smirked and said nothing until Tayja asked a question as they were turning onto Pine Tree Court, the long, serpentine driveway parking lot that snaked its way between the numerous low-income apartment buildings that made up Southgate Apartments.

"Didn't you just get a big movie deal with MTN films?" Tayja asked the question as she tapped a roll of ash from the burning end of her cigarette. "You shouldn't be out here shooting guns, Markio. What you should be doing is sitting in the back of this big, sexy ass truck with two or three cars full of shooters trailing behind you, and it should be their jobs to do all the dirty work. You're the plug now, Markio. A boss. A millionaire. Leave that gangsta shit alone and stick to writing those books. That's your ticket out of all this bullshit."

"A chief can never fully lead if he don't do no soldiering," Markio said, quoting Louisville rapper EST Gee. "Geeski said that shit on one of those albums, and it couldn't have been more true. I'll never ask one of my people to do some shit I wouldn't do my damn self. These niggas done shot my lil nigga, AJ, shot my nigga, Snoop. I can't go like that. It's gon be blood on these streets. That's it; that's all."

Tayja snickered. "You are so fucking crazy." She sucked on her cigarette. "I like that shit though. You ain't changed one bit. I'll never forget that night you came through 10th Street in that green Intrepid and shot up the crowd. KG was so mad about Dominique getting shot. You almost shot him too, but Dominique was his lil boo back then."

"They had just shot me the day before that," Markio said, thinking back to the 2005 shootings. "When the detectives came to my hospital room, I kept it solid. Told em I ain't know shit. But when I spun through there on them, they went straight to the police station. Bitch ass niggas."

The side of Tayja's pretty mouth rose into an amused smirk as she pulled back the white, leather curtain over her window and peered out at the buildings just as they were passing the staircase to a woman named Tasha's apartment. Tasha was from Gary, Indiana, 5th and Madison. Like Tayja, Tasha and her family were all Joka Mobb GDs, including the two men who were walking up the steps to her front door.

The men were Big G and Pimp, Tasha's older brother and nephew respectively. They were dressed in heavy leather Pelle Pelle jackets over designer jeans and winter boots. Tasha's daughter, Lyric, was standing inside the storm door, waiting on the two men to reach the top of the staircase. Her eyes lit up when she saw the snow-white Cullinan come rolling past. No one had ever driven through Southgate in a brand-new Rolls Royce, let alone a half million-dollar Cullinan.

Tayja buzzed her window down an inch and was just about to shout out at her fellow Gangster Disciples (or perhaps just to yell something to Pimp, with whom she shared a child), but suddenly she gasped and moved away from her window as she caught sight of the black Mercedes sedan she'd seen speeding off after the west side shooting.

Markio saw it too. It was parked right where the GPS said it would be. Near the rear of Southgate Apartments. Second court on the right. The staircase it sat facing led up to two different apartments, their doors side by side. A young, Black woman hurried down the steps, bundled up in a thick overcoat. She was carefully rolling a baby stroller down the salt covered steps. The toddler walking close behind her moved just as cautiously. She and her two children were the only tenants outside in her court.

"There go that Benz right there," Slime said, pointing one long forefinger at Voltaire's luxury sedan. "Don't look like nobody in it though."

The Benz's tinted windows were impossible to see through, but Markio knew there was nobody inside it. The car wasn't running, which meant the heat wasn't running, and it was cold outside. Aside from that, there was likely blood all over the back seats. No one liked sitting around a bunch of blood.

Markio had Apple pull into the court and stop right behind the Benz. He shouted for the woman with the stroller, and she walked over to Tayja's window with a warm smile on her narrow, brown face, her eyes darting from left to right as she took in the view of Markio's luxury SUV. He peeled off a hundred-dollar bill and pushed it through the slender opening in Tayja's window.

"This yours if you tell me who pulled up in that Benz," he said. The girl didn't hesitate.

"I forget his name, but his brother's a pro football player. He was with Eva Clarrett. They went in Dejane's apartment for a minute, then they left out with her and walked around to the back of the building. I'm guessing to somebody else's apartment. Dejane lives right there, next door to me." The girl looked from Markio to Tayja and back to Markio again. "Ain't you Millionaire Markio? The author?"

Markio only smirked. He handed her the hundred, and she did a little happy dance.

"Oh, my God, I love your books! I just finished reading *The Bird Man* series, and I just bought *Stompers* on my Kindle tablet. You are so fucking good at what you do. I'm Iyanna by the way. Can I get a pic with you?"

"Uh, no!" Tayja said snappishly. "The fuck?! Bitch, take that lil money and go on about cho business. It's real shit going on out here, and yo lil, stupid ass tryna get a picture. Get on before you get spit on."

The girl appeared hurt. She gave Tayja a contemptuous side eye. Tayja picked up her Glock, and the girl quickly turned and went back to her children on the sidewalk.

"So, what now?" Apple asked.

"We wait," Markio said, closing his right hand around the handle of his mini-Draco. "Pull over there and park. When that nigga come outside, he gets it."

Chapter 17

The apartments on the back sides of the red, brick buildings in Southgate were relatively small one bedrooms. The individual apartments consisted of a single bedroom, a utility room, one full bathroom, a linen closet, a decent sized living room, a dining area, and a slightly cramped kitchen.

Ava's boyfriend, Flocka, rented the one Eva and Voltaire had fled to. Flocka and his cousin, Benji, sold drugs out of the apartment — weed and pills and a lot of crystal meth. The two cousins had arrived with Ava and Joselyn in Ava's Jeep about three minutes after Voltaire parked his Mercedes in front of Dejane's place, and now, everyone was in the living room, seated on the faux leather sofa, the boys rolling fat blunts of exotic marijuana, the girls chattering about their mother's brazen kidnapping.

"Markio had Mama kidnapped," Eva said decidedly. "Voltaire confronted him about it, and he didn't deny it at all." She balled her hands into fists and clenched her teeth indignantly. "I wish Voltaire could've killed him."

"No," Ava said, shaking her head. "There's no way Markio had anything to do with that. He loves Mama way too much. I can't even begin to think he'd do something like that."

"Well, you need to start thinking it," Eva shot back. "That fuck nigga did it. That's why I'm glad Shotta Zoe shot his punk ass friend. Fuck them niggas. They can all die and burn in hell as far as I'm concerned."

Voltaire sat forward on the sofa. He had changed into his second set of designer gear because the first one was blood smeared from when he'd carried Shotta Zoe to the emergency room entrance. He had his gold-handled machete standing against the sofa next to his leg, and his AR pistol was stuck down in the corner of his seat cushion.

"The ex-boy will die," he said, flicking open his Zippo lighter to strike a flame at the end of his blunt. "No question there. Only questions is when." He looked at his diamond watch. "I have a flight to Miami scheduled for midnight. My people are already on the way there with millions of dollars' worth of product. We'll catch up with the ex-boy, and until then, we'll eat."

The conversation about Markio continued, but Flocka didn't say a word. Neither did Benji. They kept glancing at each other every couple of seconds, the two of them clearly pondering the quarter million dollar bounty Markio had put on Voltaire's head.

Flocka was a dope boy on the come up. He'd gone from having just a few thousand dollars in his pocket to having close to forty grand stashed away in Ava's closet safe. Three of his boys from Evansville — A1, Neekin, and Rat Face — had joined him in Michigan City a few weeks ago, and they'd been selling his dope in Lakeland Projects while he trapped out of Southgate. He'd purchased an old school Chevy Impala and put it in the shop to be painted and customized to his liking. Ava had given him twelve grand of her own money to put into the glossy blue paint job, the high-tech sound system, and the ostrich skin seats. When the winter passed, he would be riding clean like all the big-time dope boys he knew in southern Indiana and Northern Kentucky.

And if he had an additional $250,000, he'd be riding even cleaner.

His guys were already stunting in Rat Face's 2018 Porsche Panamera. Rat Face had taken his Forgiato rims off for the winter, but his SUV had a custom chameleon paint job that flipped ten different colors.

Neekin's BMW X5 was in the same custom detailing shop as Flocka's Impala, undergoing some of the same alterations. He and Rat Face were ahead of Flocka financially — they'd robbed an armored truck employee in Louisville for over two hundred grand as the man was refilling an ATM with cash — but neither of them had Flocka's hustle. They lacked the grit and determination that was needed to become real ballers. Flocka sold them pounds of meth and exotic bud that he himself purchased from other dope boys at a cheaper price. It was how he was able to stack his savings while simultaneously financing his somewhat expensive lifestyle.

The girls flitted off to the kitchen to talk amongst themselves, while Voltaire told Benji about his younger brother, Keondre Muck, and Keondre's Denver Broncos teammates. Rat Face and A1 knocked at the door a few minutes later. Flocka got up to let them in, and he immediately became jealous at the subtle and not so subtle smiles his two close friends received from the girls as they swaggered into the living room flashing their gold teeth and carrying half dozen bags of KFC meals and bottles of hard liquor.

How the fuck am I the leader and these niggas got more money than me? Flocka pondered, pushing the door shut and locking it. He noted the icy glare Voltaire aimed at his boys, but he was too frustrated to make anything of it. He shot one last glance at the Clarrett girls and their friend, Dejane, gritted his teeth when he saw the excited glow in their eyes as they returned to the living room and studied the cognac bottles A1 was placing on the table, and then he excused himself to the bathroom.

As soon as he closed the door, he took out his phone and scrolled through the list of contacts, searching for a number he'd stolen from Ava's phone.

***

The ugly, beak nose man called Rat Face stared at Eva and Ava like they were beef tenderloins, and he hadn't eaten in weeks. His gold teeth twinkled in a conniving little grin that somehow made him look even more fiendish. He wore a dark blue, leather, Givenchy jacket with a black, fur collar, Balmain jeans, Balenciaga sneakers, and a gold Rolex watch. He had cornrows that appeared freshly greased and braided, and he smelled like new money.

The heavier man introduced himself as A1. He was dressed in similar fashion, though he gave off a more cowardly aura when he reached out to dap Voltaire. He eyed the fat diamond Cuban link necklace wrapped around Voltaire's neck and all the sparkling diamonds on Voltaire's wrists and fingers.

"You like what you see?" Voltaire asked, just barely repressing his irritation.

A1 nodded, and his chin jiggled. "Hell yeah. Man, I saw you at the ESPYs with your brother last year. You was fresh as hell. Ain't he the highest paid running back in the league?"

The fat man's eyes were still lingering on Voltaire's jewelry, so Voltaire gave him a simple nod and said nothing. In his peripheral, Voltaire could see that the girls were hugging Rat Face and rummaging through the bags he and his corpulent friend had brought in.

"Damn, bro," A1 said, unable to keep himself from admiring the blinging pendant that spelled out Voltaire's name in white VVS diamonds. "How much you pay for that necklace? I know that medallion alone had to run you at least a few hundred thousand."

The fat man reached out to lift the pendant from Voltaire. In one fluid motion, he picked up his machete and swung it downward. The blade sliced right through A1's chubby, brown fingers, taking them off at the second knuckles.

A1's eyes went wide, and he unleashed a blood-curdling scream as his severed fingers went tumbling across the stained brown carpet. Voltaire snapped to his feet and shoved A1 in the chest, sending him falling over the coffee table. At the same time, Voltaire turned to Rat Face and delivered a devastating blow to his head, burying the blade in the poor man's hideous face from the right brow to the left side of his mouth and cutting his nose in two. Voltaire snatched the blade loose, and Rat Face dropped to his knees, holding both hands to the grisly wound; all four of the teenage girls screamed out in horror, and Benji's eyes bulged from their sockets.

"Reach for my chain?! Are you out your mind?!" Voltaire exclaimed heatedly.

"I ain't mean no disrespect, man," A1 said, his voice cracking a time or two. "Aww, shit. Aww, shit! You cut my fucking fingers off!"

Benji flipped over the rear of the sofa, and the girls went scrambling into the kitchen as Voltaire reached for his AR pistol.

"You never reach for a gangster's chain," he said, spinning around to confront A1. "Never.'

He raised the gun and pointed the long silencer at A1's fleshy brown forehead. A1 raised his blood-soaked hands to block his face, and three or four bullets spiraled through his palms, through his nose and mouth, and out the back of his head. The high caliber rifle rounds carved round holes in the carpeted floor before A1 slumped over, dead.

Voltaire swung the gun over to Rat Face and shot the young man multiple times in the side of the head without even looking directly at him. He then turned his attention to the spot on the sofa where Benji had been seated. Seeing that the seat was now vacant, he shifted his frigid gaze to the girls in the kitchen, trying to see if Benji was in there with them, and as soon as he looked that way, the front door flew open behind him. He spun and aimed just in time to glimpse the back of Benji's jogger as the teenage boy threw open the storm door and vanished from sight.

Dejane was running out of the kitchen when Voltaire turned back to study the girls. She had a frightened expression painted on her pretty, brown face, and her waist length, purple braids seemed to float behind her as she ran toward him. He let her sprint past him, and then he fired at the back of her head and watched her fall against the open front door and slide down to the floor.

"You three come with me," Voltaire said to Whitney's daughters.

The three Clarrett girls followed his orders, sobbing uncontrollably and sticking close to one another as they entered the living room. Voltaire slipped his machete into his duffle bag and lifted the bag by its straps. Then thinking of Ava's boyfriend, he rushed over to the closed bathroom door and sent fifteen rounds through it. He heard a groan and the dull thud of Flocka hitting the floor, and he briefly considered kicking in the door to finish him off, but then he remembered that Benji was outside somewhere, possibly seeking police assistance, so he emptied the remainder of his fifty round banana clip into the lower part of the door, where he though Flocka might have landed, and without waiting to hear anything more, he fled the apartment with the Clarrett girls in tow.

***

The first bullet wound was on the lower left side of Flocka's sharply defined abdomen. The second round had taken the top two inches off his right hand's thumb, and the third one had blasted through slabs of muscle in his left thigh.

Stunned by the chaotic screams and muffled gunfire he'd heard from the living room a few seconds ago, he had already drawn and cocked his 9-millimeter Ruger pistol.

Still, the shots through the door had caught him off guard, and before he knew it, his body was stinging from the gunshot wounds.

Panicking, he fell to the floor and immediately crawled to the bathtub and climbed over into it, staring up at the ceiling with his eyes wide and his chest rising and falling in rapid succession. His AirPods were in his ears. He'd been on the line with Markio, telling the wealthy, older man where he could find Voltaire, but now, Flocka kept his lips sealed as another nearly silent spray of bullets raked across the door.

"What the fuck was that?' Markio asked.

Flocka didn't reply. Instead, he sat up and pointed his gun at the bullet riddled door. But there was no one there. He could see clear through the splintered holes into the short hallway beyond, and there was nobody out there.

"Flocka?" Markio probed.

"It was him. Voltaire." Wincing, Flocka checked the gushing hole in his stomach. "Shit. I'm shot. That nigga just tried to kill me."

Chapter 18

Markio knitted his brow and ended the call with Flocka. He looked over at Tayja and forward at Apple and Slime. He'd had the call on speaker. Everyone had heard the entirety of his conversation with Flocka. They all knew that Voltaire was inside an apartment directly behind the building his Benz was parked in front of and that someone had screamed out about their fingers cut off and that Voltaire had just shot Flocka. Apparently, that was all of the information Slime needed because he looked back at Markio, nodded twice, and then threw open his door and took off toward the building with his green Gucci bandana tied around his face and his mini-Draco held low at his side.

"You want me out there too?" Apple asked.

Markio shook his head no. "Nah, you and Tayja stay in here. I'll be right back."

He exited his rear suicide door with his own mini-Draco in hand and went to his driver's window to get Apple's red ski mask before pulling it down over his head and running toward the opposite side of the apartment building. Iyanna and her toddler watched him as he made it onto the sidewalk and headed for the concrete steps that led down and around to the one-bedroom apartments at the back.

He never made it to the snow packed concrete steps.

Joselyn came rushing up those same steps before Markio had even made it to the portion of sidewalk that branched off to the side of the building. Eva and Ava were right behind her, their eyes and mouth agape.

And then came Voltaire.

The Haitian man was jogging up the steps with a duffle bag hanging from one brawny shoulder and an AR pistol with an attached sound suppressor clutched in one hand. He and Markio locked eyes like two mature male rams preparing to butt heads. Voltaire let his duffle bag slip down from his shoulder and land heavily beside him, and he glowered at Markio as he positioned both of his herculean hands on his AR pistol. Markio stopped in his tracks and reciprocated with his own icy stare.

They lifted their guns simultaneously, and Markio got off the first couple of shots. He moved to his left, and as he did it, he re-entered the parking lot to take cover beside a dark green Kia Telluride. He expected Voltaire to return fire, but the big man only aimed his AR pistol at Markio and then turned to run back in the direction from which he'd came. It was then that Markio realized Voltaire must have emptied his clip inside Flocka's apartment.

Markio rose and aimed and fired. The gunshots made his ears ring. Fire belched from the short barrel of his mini-Draco pistol. At least one round pounded through the back of Voltaire's left shoulder. The impact jerked Voltaire forward, and he lost his footing on an icy patch of ground.

The slip proved fatal.

Voltaire went down on one knee, and before he could rise again, Slime was standing over him with the mini-Draco aimed at his forehead. A quick three round burst was all it took to blast half of Voltaire's head off his neck. He toppled over into a three-foot high pile of snow.

Running back to his Cullinan, Markio caught a fleeting glimpse of the Clarrett girls as they hopped in Ava's red Jeep Grand Cherokee. He also saw that Iyanna had ripped her infant child from inside the stroller and was hurrying up the steps to her apartment, dragging her toddler along behind her.

As soon as Markio and Slime were seated in the Cullinan, Apple made a hasty U-turn and fled the apartment complex behind Ava's SUV, only Ava went one way and Apple went the other. A few minutes later, they were back on Interstate 94, racing off toward Chicago.

Markio snatched off the red ski mask and rubbed his waves back into place. He concealed his mini-Draco in his duffle bag and dropped it over the back of his seat. Apple turned on some music — Twista's classic street anthem *Adrenaline Rush* —and for a while, they all rode in silence, their eyes vigilantly studying every passing vehicle.

It wasn't until Markio's phone rang with a call from Nikkia that he realized Tayja was still seated beside him.

"This my girl calling," he said.

Tayja sucked her teeth. "Boy, I know the game. I ain't gon say shit."

Markio cracked a grin. His heart was drumming in his chest. His hands were tremulous with adrenaline. He answered the FaceTime call from Nikkia and tried to put on a genuine smile as her gorgeous, brown visage appeared on his phone screen.

Nikkia wasn't smiling. In fact, she was outright scowling.

Chapter 19

Lil Luke's stepmother, Pandy, had come through for him yet again. He'd texted her saying he had the woman of his dreams sitting in his living room but that he was running low on cash, and twenty minutes later, a chubby, southside girl named Cherrelle pulled up in front of his Trumbull Avenue home in a blacked-out Range Rover. The cute, big girl had handed Lil Luke a thick pile of hundreds before bidding him farewell and cruising off down the block.

Back in the house, he'd slapped Noesha across the face with the stack of cash, and she'd snatched him by the collar of his shirt, biting down on her bottom lip and showing a combative expression that made her look even sexier to him.

"Don't get fucked up, boy," she said.

"I might like that shit," he replied, slipping an arm around her narrow waist to grab a handful of her fat, bouncy ass. The others had laughed at the dramatic show of attraction, and Noesha, still clutching the collar of Lil Luke's thousand-dollar shirt, had walked off toward the hallway that led to the bedroom.

Now, just ten minutes later, Noesha was on her back on Lil Luke's luxurious king size bed, naked from the waist down, with her fingers tangled in the curly ropes of his dreads as he slipped two fingers in and out of her while treating her engorged clitoris to a series of wet and gentle licks.

To Lil Luke, she tasted like honey. He was high off Percs and weed and buzzing off the cognac they'd consumed, and the sight of her creamy juices on his pistoning fingers had his dick as hard as the Glock pistol on his hip.

When he started to move up on his knees, Noesha tightened her grip on his dreads and knitted her brow as she looked down at him.

"What are you doing?" Noesha asked, her tone replete with attitude.

"Finna fuck the life outta yo lil thick ass," Lil Luke said, taking a ribbed condom from his left-hand pocket.

"Nuh uh. You gotta make me cum first."

It was Lil Luke's turn to furrow his brow, but then, he smirked, licked his lips, nodded his head, and went back to work on her pussy, sucking and licking on her clitoris while jamming his fingers inside her to the hilt.

Despite the drugs coursing through his system, Lil Luke's mind was working quite well. Jackboy and Ricky, two of his fellow TVLs, had arrived half an hour ago, and now they were out in the living room with Jaybo, Lacey, and Quita. They'd spoken with Lil Luke and Jaybo in private about Travis' murder and what they would do to retaliate. The police had 13th and Sawyer on lock right now, but they wouldn't be there for long. Jackboy and Ricky were carrying two of the illegally modified Glocks the gang had gotten from Millionaire Markio. Jackboy had a fifty round drum magazine on it.

Lil Luke began to hear another feminine moan coming from outside of his bedroom. Sheisty Lord had a bitch in his bed just about every day. They treated their shared residence like a bachelor pad, and together, they'd slain the vast majority of promiscuous women their neighborhood had to offer.

But Noesha was different. In Lil Luke's opinion, none of those other girls had anything on her. He spread her vaginal lips apart to lap up the trickling juices as she held the back of his head and moaned repeatedly, and then, he continued his merciless attack on her rigid little clitoris, sucking and licking and blowing on it, rubbing his fingertips across it — anything to make her cum.

He got what he wanted five minutes later when she balled his dreads in her fists and spasmed against his dripping mouth. He felt only a hint of pain from her tight grasp on his hair. The Percocets and cognac he'd ingested dulled the ache to almost nothing.

"Mmmmmm," Noesha moaned.

It was the sexiest sound Lil Luke had ever heard.

When she finally freed his locs from her small, delicate fists, Lil Luke rose up on his knees and hastily tore open the condom with his teeth. He whipped out his nine-inch erection and stroked it in one hand.

Noesha gawked at the intimidating length and girth of his dick. "Oh, my God," she said.

"God ain't got nothin to do with it," Lil Luke replied. He snatched his shirt over his head, rolled the condom onto his concrete hard pole, and rubbed the bulbous head up and down between the warm, lubricious folds of Noesha's labia. "I'm about to break yo lil, thick ass in half, Noesha, on my dead homies."

Little did Lil Luke know, he was just a few minutes away from having another dead homie to swear upon, and he would hear every deadly clap of gunfire.

Chapter 20

Skip hadn't gone to the airport.

Tammy had tried taking him there. "You need to listen to your uncle and get the fuck outta Chicago," she said as they careened down Kedzie Avenue. "You just killed that boy, and Travis ain't just anybody. He's a real deal factor. His people ain't gon let that go. You gon have the police on yo ass, and you gon have the Travelers on yo ass. That's a bad combination."

It was good advice, but Skip had ignored it just the same. He'd phoned Meatball, and four minutes after the shooting, he had Tammy pull up next to Meatball's gray Dodge Caravan in the alleyway on 16th and Lawndale Avenue. He handed her the two hundred dollars he'd intended to pay for an hour of intimacy and told her he'd catch up with her later, and then, he got out of her SUV and joined the gang in the minivan.

Now, he was in another alleyway. Meatball had been riding around, looking for the blue Ford Explorer full of hoodrats that had sped off after the shooting, and they'd found it parked in a vacant lot on Trumbull Avenue. Now, they were parked in the alley one house over from the vacant lot, watching the SUV like vultures over a dying animal.

"You hit that nigga up, G," Karo said, looking over at Skip with a proud smirk on his handsome, light brown face. "I couldn't believe that shit. I was just telling Hank that shorty had a lot of nerve pullin up in the hood after Pojo and

Elise had just got shot down there on Christiana and look what happened to his dumb ass."

"Pojo gon be proud of you," Meatball said, nodding his large, bald head and drumming his fingers on the steering wheel. "You stood on business for bro. Laid that nigga, Travis, down like a pallet. No hesitation."

Skip kept his mouth shut and his gaze fixed on the tattoo he had on the back of his left hand. "R.I.P. Cash Boy," it read in purple and yellow lettering because the Los Angeles Lakers had always been his older brother, Cash Boy's favorite NBA team. Now that his other older brother had been shot and nearly killed by a member of the same gang that had killed Cash Boy, he felt it was only right that he retaliated. His mother wouldn't be the only Black woman crying her eyes out on this cold winter day.

He closed his hand around the butt of his Mac 12 and drew in a breath. He raised his eyes to stare at the Explorer as Big Hank tried calling one of the girls for the umpteenth time since Skip had joined them.

"This bitch still ain't pickin up," Hank said after a time. "On fo'nem grave, if I find out she over here with one of them Travelers, I'm stompin her ears together."

The mental image of Hank stomping some girl's head flat elicited a brief chuckle from Skip. "G, you crazy as hell," he said, shaking his head.

"Man," Meatball asked, "why Steel always be calling Cash Boy his son?"

Skip regarded Meatball with a hard look. "He ain't never called my brother his son. That's our uncle."

"On Instagram this morning, when he was getting on that nigga, Markio, about Cash Boy getting killed, he called Cash Boy his son," Meatball explained. "And when he was in the joint with my uncle, he told him the same thing. He said his son got killed, not his nephew."

Beside Skip, Karo stifled a laugh. Skip thought the laughter might have come out in full had he not been holding the gun he'd just used to kill Travis McCall. The sight of it seemed to make Karo think twice about enjoying a laugh at Skip's expense.

"Yo gay ass uncle don't know what the fuck he talking about," Skip said. His expression became twisted in a threateningly belligerent mug, and he switched to a different topic. "What's up with these hoes? Why in the fuck is they over here in the first place? They fucking with the opps?'

It was a good question. Meatball shrugged his broad shoulders and adjusted his black and gray Bulls skullcap, pulling it down over his ears.

"The bitches ain't answering the phone," he said. "I done called Lacey eleven times back-to-back, and she ain't picked up yet. We was s'posed to be on our way to a hotel party."

"That bitch, Lacey, so bad," Karo said, groping himself as he bit down on the middle of his bottom lip and groaned lustfully. "And her buddy, Noesha, even badder than her. Shit, her whole squad bad. Hank fucked Quita on my couch the other night, and Meatball had Lacey hemmed up in my laundry room. The lil bitch, Noesha, wouldn't give me no play though. You can tell she one of them money hungry bitches. If you ain't breakin bread, she ain't givin up no pussy. Point blank period."

Skip knew exactly who Noesha Long was. She was one of the baddest bitches on the west side of Chicago, and her friends were just as stunningly attractive. Everybody followed them on social media. Aside from Bankroll Reese's fiancée, Shawnna Wilkins, and her identical twin, Dawn, and Lakita "Bubbles" Thomas, the mouthwateringly thick former stripper who'd married the Wilkins' twins' father, Juice, Noesha and her buddies were the baddest bitches on the west side of the city.

Not that Skip cared one way or another. He was an unemployed, ugly son of a bitch who rarely ever had any money. He was accustomed to getting himself off with a jar of Vaseline and a Pornhub video. He liked to watch big bootied, Brazilian girls taking huge, black dicks up their darkly puckered assholes; every time he jacked off watching one of those videos, his curved, ten-inch length of meat would harden and eject bubbly white ropes of semen up to five feet away. The few beautiful women he'd been fortunate enough to bed had all come with a fee — as was the case with most bad bitches nowadays — and since he'd never been all that great at hustling, he usually ended up dicking down the women that didn't accumulate hundreds of likes on their Facebook photos, the women who worked at fast food joints and babysat and did hair in their kitchens, the mediocre women who pined for a grimy, young, Black man with a girthy ten inch tool to stretch them open every now and then.

One of those women was Shaquana, a fat, dark skinned girl from the east side of Chicago he'd been fucking since last Juneteenth. She was a waitress at Tinky's Bar and Grill on 16th Street. He'd texted her shortly after he killed Travis.

"Where u @? I need u," he'd messaged.

Two minutes later, she'd texted back. "Just got off work. Why? Wussup?"

"U know where 2 find Lil Luke?"

"Don't know a Lil Luke," she'd texted back, and thirty seconds after that, she'd messaged him again. "Wait, do you mean Luke the Producer's son? If so, I believe he stays somewhere on Trumbull. He's the one who got locked up for that double murder @ Tamia's apt when Chandra and Marshall got killed."

This particular thread of text messages was the reason Skip had urged Meatball to ride down Trumbull. A millisecond before he'd ducked for cover in that Christiana Avenue alleyway, Skip had caught a fleeting glimpse of Lil Luke popping out of the black Dodge Charger Hellcat with a pistol in hand and opening fire on Elise's windshield. He'd slithered down from his seat until he was curled in a fetal position on the floorboard, and he'd looked up and watched the bullets tear through his brother's broad chest.

The indelible memory of that traumatizing shooting played in his mind on a perpetual loop, and now that he was looking at the very same black Dodge Charger Hellcat parked just behind the blue Ford Explorer in the vacant lot beside 1530 South Trumbull Avenue, he couldn't help clenching his teeth and glowering at the Charger as he waited for Lil Luke to make an appearance.

"On my dead brother," he said, twisting his neck until it made a sharp crackling sound, "the first nigga I catch walking toward that Charger getting stretched."

Chapter 21

Ricky Cross was a certified lame; there was no other way to accurately describe him. He always seemed to say and do all the wrong things, and quite often, he found himself being the butt of the joke when the gang was in need of a good laugh. In fact, if not for his older cousin, Ceno, being one of the only rap artists from the area to attain a notable level of success in the music industry, he knew for certain that the little bit of love and respect he got from all the local niggas and hood bitches would be history.

That being said, he wasn't at all surprised to find himself sitting in an armchair in Lil Luke and Sheisty Lord's living room while Jackboy and Jaybo dicked down the tall girl who'd introduced herself to them as Lacey.

The other girl, Shaquita Hales — Ricky knew her full name because he followed her on TikTok and Instagram — stood smiling down at the threesome with her phone in hand, recording video of her friend, Lacey, who was on all fours on the sofa, getting fucked from behind by Jackboy while Jaybo supported himself on one knee in front of her sloppy, wet mouth. Jackboy had paid Lacey four hundred dollars to bust it open for him and Jaybo, and she'd gotten right to it, digging a box of condoms out of her purse and passing one to each of the two young men.

Ricky had been watching Lacey get fucked for over ten minutes now. His dick was as hard as a baseball bat. He adjusted it in his jeans and released a sigh of sexual frustration. He reached out to grope Quita's fat, round globe of an ass and received a swift smack on the hand for the transgression.

"Boy, you need to stop," she said, turning to him with a sour look on her sexy, brown face. "I'm sorry but ain't nothing about you that turns me on. You can keep your hands to yourself. Thank you very much."

"I'll let you sit on my face right now."

"I just bet you would," Quita said with a disgusted roll of the eyes.

Two minutes later, Jaybo reached over to the coffee table and grabbed the electronic key to Lil Luke's Dodge Charger. He tossed it to Ricky and said, "Bro, go out there and grab me that jar of zah out the glove compartment. I forgot I left it in there."

A "jab" was a bundle of drugs that had already been packaged for distribution, and "zah" was short for exotic marijuana. Right about now, Ricky needed a blunt of something strong, so he took the key and left out the front door with his head lowered defeatedly.

The cold air hit him like a bucket of ice water as soon as he stepped out onto the front porch, and an ancient Oldsmobile Delta 88 went trundling past the house as he was descending the ice slick concrete steps. He recognized the driver as Crunchy, a TVL from Leamington Avenue's "Wicked Town" faction. Crunchy was a robber who Ricky had known for years, so he knew the car was probably stolen and that Crunchy was likely only passing through the hood to off load some confiscated merchandise. Crunchy had never tried to rob any of the gang members in Ricky's neighborhood, but Ricky and the other Vice Lords in Holy City were watchful of him nonetheless.

Ricky watched the car until it turned onto 15th Street and disappeared from view. Then, he continued on toward Lil Luke's blacked out Charger, pausing briefly to admire the rims and candy paint on Sheisty Lord's orange Impala. The snow that blanketed the vacant lot crunched noisily beneath his Air Jordan 3s. He took out his phone and went to xvideos.com as he approached the Charger, and by the time he unlocked the doors and slipped into the driver's seat, he was already on a porn video that showed adult film star Trey Shongz lying on his back in bed while a petite, young redbone rode his face.

After turning on the heat, Ricky shot a quick glance at his surroundings and then wrestled his seven-inch erection out of his jeans. Lil Luke had parked facing the alleyway that ran between Trumbull and St. Louis Avenue. A teenage girl was carrying a heavy bag of garbage to the trash can behind her family's garage, and there was a minivan parked behind another house. Ricky saw a movement inside the minivan, but since they were so far away, he paid them no mind for there was no way either passenger would be able to see him, especially not after he reclined in the driver's seat, which was exactly what he did not even a full minute after pulling the driver door shut and keying the ignition to get the heat going.

Stroking his dick in one hand while holding his smartphone in the other, he looked around for something to shoot his load into and found nothing. He stopped masturbating long enough to pop open the glove compartment and take out the jab of weed and an old McDonald's napkin, and then he went to work, jacking his dick and watching the porno, imagining that it was him lying there with Shaquita Hales riding his face. Every few seconds, he'd sit up to look around and make sure there was no one approaching him, then his eyes would return to the video, and he'd go back to thinking about Quita.

After another minute or so, he shoved his jeans all the way down to his ankles and jacked his dick as rapidly as he could.

"Yeah. That pussy taste so good, Quita. Mm," Ricky muttered, licking his chapped lips as he listened to the low, sexy moans of the beautiful, young woman whose pussy Trey Shlongz was slurping to high heaven. He envisioned Quita's orgasmic nectar dripping down onto his steadily flickering tongue and tried to imagine how arousing her sexual moans would sound and how delectable her vaginal juices would taste.

He was nearing a volcanic eruption when the unexpected sound of an approaching vehicle jarred him from his imagination. His eyes popped open, and he sat up just as the gray minivan came skidding to a stop along the passenger's side of the Charger.

Ricky's brow came together as his rattled mind attempted to come up with an explanation for what his stunned eyes were seeing. At the same time, he reached down to pull up his pants and boxers. He'd placed his pistol on the passenger's seat, but he didn't think to reach for it until the minivan's sliding door came open, and Skip leapt out, aiming a submachine gun right at him.

And by then, it was too late for Ricky to do much of anything. He was reaching for his .40 caliber Glock 23 when the Mac in Skip's hands flashed and boomed several times in a row. Four or five holes appeared in the passenger's side window, and suddenly, he found himself slumped against his door with a number of stinging bullet wounds in his neck, shoulders, and chest. He managed to cast a glance downward and saw that one round had plowed through the head of his exposed erection — beheading it so to speak. And then, Skip's gun flashed again, and Ricky's troubled soul shot right out of his body.

Chapter 22

Nikkia set in on Markio as soon as he answered the video call. "I hope you know you just lost a really good woman," she snapped, switching to her rear camera, so he could see that her billionaire friend, Alexus Costilla-King, was seated across from her on the gulf stream private jet. "I'm sure you know by now that there isn't very much that gets past her. She has people who know people in every city, every social circle, every organization, every government agency. And guess what? Do you know the woman you had your cousin, Tito, give your phone number to behind my back last night? I'd like you to take one wild guess at who she works for."

Markio's eyebrows had risen in alarm, and he'd said, "What? She with the police or some'n?"

"Try the Federal Bureau of Investigation," Nikkia retorted. "Teresa Dunlap is FBI Agent Deborah Wade. She's building a case against you and your gang, and you were brilliant enough to offer her your phone number."

"I only gave her my number because she was one of my fans. At least that's what she claimed to be."

"So, basically, you're telling me that every bitch who reads your books can get your personal phone number now? Is that what you're saying?"

"I had just signed a book for her in VIP, and I figured, you know, with her shape and all, I might be able to use her for a future book cover. On Neal, that's all it was."

Nikkia had rolled her eyes and sucked her teeth, and in that instance, Markio saw the hood chick she'd been before she became a world-famous attorney.

"You're in a relationship with me, and yet you went out of your way to give another woman your phone number. That tells me all I need to know."

She'd ended the call right then and there. That was fifty-three minutes ago, just as his Rolls Royce Cullinan was merging onto Interstate 94. He was already back on the west side of Chicago, now having phoned Nikkia several times during the road trip. She wasn't picking up.

One person who had picked up was Ava Clarrett. She'd answered the FaceTime call, regarded him with an untrusting, accusatory scowl, and then ended the video call without voicing a single word.

The time now was 7:20 p.m. Markio was staring out his window and listening to NBA YoungBoy's *Colors* album (Jarvon had pressed play on the album five minutes earlier, and now, Youngboy's *Bring It On* was blaring from the Cullinan's sound system) as Apple cruised down 16th Street. They'd stopped on Christiana just long enough for three of his fellow gang members — Tweet Body, Bay-Bay, and Kion — to load up into Tweet Body's plum colored BMW X7, and now, they were driving westbound, just crossing Homan Avenue.

Markio had just realized that his cousin, Jarvon, and NBA YoungBoy sounded almost exactly alike when a series of distant gunshots emptied his mind of the thought.

Apple swung his head around for a quick glance at Markio; Slime snatched his mini-Draco from under his thigh, and Tayja, who'd somehow managed to nod off in the comfortable leather seat, came to with wide eyes and immediately dug in her purse for her pistol.

"Pay attention to the road, nigga," Markio said to Apple. His own mini-Draco lay next to him on the armrest. He picked it up, leaned forward, and stared straight ahead just as a gray minivan came speeding out of the alleyway between Trumbull and St. Louis.

The Dodge Caravan made a swift right turn onto 16th Street, coming perilously close to colliding with a CTA bus that was passing the mouth of the alley at that very moment. Markio knew right away that the minivan was occupied by the opposition. He'd spoken with his old friend, Luke Duke, aka Big Duke, not even twenty minutes ago. Big Luke had learned from a woman named Pinky that the New Breeds had told her to keep her mouth shut about Travis' murder and that her cousin, Scooter, had just seen Steel's nephew, Skip, getting into Meatball's gray minivan.

The minivan's tires skidded on the wet street and made a sharp left turn onto St. Louis Avenue. At the same time, a CPD squad car activated the sirens, darted around from somewhere behind Markio's SUV, and shot off down 16th in hot pursuit of the fleeing Caravan.

"What the hell is going on?" Tayja asked no one in particular.

Markio gave her no response. He looked at Slime and said, "That was them niggas who killed my guy, Big Keanan's lil brother earlier today."

"I think they might've just shot somebody on Trumbull," Apple said. He had slowed to a stop at the corner of 16th and Trumbull and flicked on the right hand turn signal.

"Go ahead and slide down Trumbull," Markio said. "Make sure Lil Luke and Sheisty ain't get hit up."

Apple made the turn and went barreling down Trumbull Avenue. Lil Luke's house was smack dab in the middle of the block on the left side of the one-way street. The Cullinan went sliding forward four more feet when Apple stomped down on the brake pedal, and when it finally came to a halt, the vantage from Markio's window was perfectly angled for him to not only see the bullet-riddled passenger's side of Lil Luke's sleek black Charger but also the three young men who were rushing out on the front porch at 1530 South Trumbull Avenue.

Lil Luke was among the three, and like the others, he was holding up his pants with one hand while gripping a Glock in the other. Markio lowered his window as Jaybo ran down the steps and through the snow to the Dodge Charger Hellcat.

"Aw shit, Joe," Jaybo shouted. He stood outside the driver door and looked in. "They shot Ricky, bruh. Shot him in the face, pushed his shit back."

Markio looked from one end of the block to the other, holding his mini-Draco in both hands, his forefinger curled over the trigger, the palm of his other hand cradling the wooden grip on the underside of the 7.62-millimeter pistol. The tension of the moment was palpable. The years' long war between the Traveling Vice Lords and the Black Gangster New Breeds was officially reignited, and once again, Markio found himself right in the thick of it. He had about $20 million to his name, yet he was in the middle of the trenches with his gang where dangers of all sorts lurked around every corner.

Most men would have folded right then and got themselves out of harm's way, but not Markio Earl. The average multimillionaire with a personal chauffer would have called it a day and told their driver to head for the home front, but Markio told Apple to circle back around to 16th Street, so they could begin their search for the gray Dodge Caravan.

The Cullinan and the X7 following it moved in a blur. North to the corner of 15th and Trumbull, east to the corner of 15th and Homan, south to the corner of 16th and Homan, and finally back onto 16th Street, heading westbound.

"I knew I should've stayed my yellow ass in Michigan City," Tayja muttered discontentedly.

"You'll be good," Markio said in his most comforting voice. "I'd die before I let anything happen to you. You know how close I was with Tristan. He might've been folks, but he was my brother too."

He didn't look at Tayja — he was much too focused on the street ahead, first eyeing a parked minivan that turned out to be a light blue Honda then squinting at a passing dark gray Kia minivan — but he could see her staring at him in his peripheral. She had that sexy smile on her angelically beautiful face again, a captivating smile that sucked all the breath from Markio's lungs. He had to force himself to focus on the task at hand.

As Apple floored it across St Louis Avenue, Markio looked to his left and gawked at the flurry of police activity about two blocks down. The New Breeds had abandoned the minivan in the middle of the street.

"Slow down up here on Drake," Markio barked, and Apple did as he was told, pressing down on the brake to slow the Cullinan as they neared the corner of 16th and Drake Avenue.

They were right on time, arriving at the corner just as two young, Black men — one of whom Markio recognized as a Breed named Hank — rounded the corner on foot and went rushing into the corner store across the street. They were clearly in a hurry; the dozen or more west side Chicagoans entering and leaving the convenience store regarded the pair with wary eyes.

"I think that was Skip right there," Apple said.

"Which one?" Slime asked.

"The shorter one who just ran in the store in front of that big nigga in the gray jacket."

Slime nodded and pushed open his door. He'd only stuck one leg out when Markio stopped him and pointed at the CPD camera that was suspended from a utility pole farther down the street.

"Pull around the corner onto Drake Avenue."

Tweet Body pulled in right behind them, but Slime was out of the Cullinan and sprinting up the sidewalk and across

16th Street before either of the X7's doors had even swung open.

Markio was pushing open his door when Tayja grabbed hold of his elbow and squeezed.

"Let them handle that," she said, holding her Glock in her other hand. Looking back, Markio saw that Tweet Body, Bay-Bay, and Kion were running behind Slime with Glocks in their hands. Everyone outside the store scattered as the four-armed gangsters came dashing toward them.

Markio's toes curled over in his Louis Vuitton shoes, and he clenched his teeth. This was the first time he'd ever even considered not shooting his gun when there was war in the streets.

"Close your door," Tayja said firmly.

Looking at Markio in the rearview mirror, Apple nodded his head and said, "Listen to that woman. She ain't telling you nothing wrong."

Reluctantly, Markio shut his door and turned in his seat to look out the back window just as a flash of gunfire lit up the convenience store's glass front door.

"You are entirely too rich for this bullshit," Tayja went on. "You should be overseas somewhere — sightseeing in Egypt, shopping in Dubai, yachting in Ibiza, anything but this."

"That's white people shit," Markio declared.

Fifteen to twenty more gunshots sounded, and suddenly, the door to the convenience store burst open. The boy Apple had identified as Skip came stumbling out, dropping to one knee and rising up again, blood pouring from his chest and limbs. Slime walked out behind him and sprayed the back of his head with 7.62-millimeter Draco rounds, and Skip fell dead on the sidewalk.

A woman's bloodcurdling scream filled the air. A teenage girl who'd been running with a toddler in her arms tripped and fell in the middle of the street, and a brown Ford pickup truck swerved to avoid turning her and her kid into twin speed bumps. Slime crossed the street like Usain Bolt at the 2012 Summer Olympics and was back in his seat seconds later. Tweet Body and Bay-Bay made it back to the X7 just as the Cullinan was rocketing off down Drake, but Kion didn't make it in time. He ran into the front end of an arriving police car and tumbled over it. His pistol went flying one way, his untied Air Force sneaker went flying in another direction, and that was the last Markio saw of him before the X7 got behind his Cullinan and blocked his view of 16th Street.

"Where we going?" Apple asked.

Markio looked over at Tayja. His adrenal glands were on fire, his finger trembled from the surge of adrenaline. He took out his iPhone, googled "5-star hotel," and clicked on the Costilla Hotel & Towers. He booked a five day stay in the Presidential Suite for $8,500 per night.

"Head downtown, gang," he said. "To the Costilla Hotel. Then, I want you to get an Uber, go home to your family, and enjoy the rest of your night. I got Slime and Tayja with me. I'll be good."

Chapter 23

"Why is it that all you young hoes do is look at those phones? It could be the end of the world, Jesus could be standing right in front of you, and you wouldn't even notice. All because of that goddamn phone."

Tammy snickered and looked up from her phone. She and Steel were in the backseat of his clean, white Nissan Rogue. The gray bearded older man was seated beside her, stroking his fat, black penis in one ashy brown fist. A globule of semen oozed out of the urethral hole in the head of his dick. Tammy lowered her head to his lap, licked the pearly white bead of cum onto the tip of her tongue, and sent it down her throat where the rest of his salty load had gone.

It had been over three hours since news of Skip's murder had reached his already distraught mother. Now, Tammy and Steel were sitting in the vast parking lot just across the road from Northwestern Memorial Hospital where Pojo was undergoing his fourth lifesaving surgery of the day. Steel and Neetra had decided against going to the airport when they learned that Skip had joined Meatball and the other Breeds in the gray minivan, so instead, they'd returned to the hospital.

Twon and Lil Sam, the younger brothers of Neetra's incarcerated husband, Big Sam, had arrived at the hospital a little over an hour ago to support their grieving sister in-law and also to promise revenge for Pojo's injuries and Skip's murder. Twon and Lil Sam were both Black Disciples from the notoriously dangerous low-end area of Chicago's south side, and like most gang members in the city, they were all too eager to put a bullet through the skull of an opposing gang member.

"Well," Tammy said, slipping her iPhone down into the side pocket of her red, leather Fendi bag. "Excuse me for being so technologically savvy. I know you're probably used to those old rotary phones, but this a new day. The age of the smartphone. I pay all my bills with the money I make from being on this phone. You did a lot of years in prison, old man. Get with the time."

"You're supposed to be focused on me right now," Steel countered, still pulling on his deflating phallus. "I ain't pay you all the money for you to look at that phone."

Tammy turned to face him, narrowing her eyes and crossing her skinny arms over her chest. She wore a red Fendi sweater with no bra underneath. Her noticeably erect nipples protruded from the rich cotton fabric, and the sweater was small enough to reveal her flat stomach and the five-carat diamond stud she'd had pierced through her belly button.

"First of all," she said, ratchetly swaying her neck from side to side, "you gave me fifty funky ass dollars. I usually charge at least a hundred for this good head, but I felt bad about what happened to Skip, so I showed you some love. Secondly, you still owe me some money for giving Skip a ride after he shot Travis. I ain't forgot about that either."

Steel licked his thick lips and smiled like a fool. He picked a fat, gray booger from his left nostril and admired it before dragging it across the thigh of his sweatpants. The sight of it made Tammy want to vomit.

"Tell me everything you know about that nigga, Markio," he said. "I need to know it all. Cause I know he the one with all the money."

"It ain't just him. You got Bankroll Reese, Bam, Cocky Lord, Perk Lord — most people call him Juice, but I know him as Perk. All them niggas is millionaires. Plus, you know they're all friends with Bulletface, and he's a fucking billionaire. Big Luke's a millionaire too. I ain't gon lie. You gon have your hands full tryna go to war with the Travelers. I grew up around them. They done killed everybody, whoever disrespected them."

Steel nibbled at his lower lip, clearly lost in an ocean deep state of contemplation. His flaccid wet penis remained in his ashy, dry fist, but he was no longer stroking it. He gazed out his window at a handsome Hispanic man who'd just climbed out of a Jaguar sedan. The man wore purple nurse's scrubs, the pants of which fit snugly on his lean, young legs, and he moved in a feminine manner that led Tammy to believe he might be gay.

When Tammy gave Steel's dick another glance, it was rock hard and standing upright in his fist, and he was jacking it again.

Tammy knitted her brow and drew back a little. *This nigga is gay as fuck,* she thought to herself and suddenly, she regretted swallowing his cum. In fact, she regretted ever going to Neetra's apartment to begin with. Skip's bum ass had been offering to trick on her for months now. She'd turned him down at least twenty times. It just so happened that when he DM'ed her earlier today, she had just finished getting her pussy sucked on for over an hour by Fendi Da Rapper's lesbian sister, and she'd been in dire need of some good dick. Skip had messaged her saying he had $200 to dick her down for an hour, and Tammy had been too horny to ignore the offer.

And besides, Tammy had never been one to turn down a check. Steel turned his head to stare at Tammy. He had a ravenous hunger in his eyes, and he was breathing harder than before. "I want you to pull down them panties and bend that ass over right here in front of me," he said. "Let me eat that booty hole. I got another fifty for you."

"Nigga, you got me fucked up," Tammy snapped, her face twisted in disgust. "Pay me what you owe me so I can go home to my daughter, and you need to be in the hospital with your sister and her son."

Steel shook his head no, and in a flash, he reached out and took hold of Tammy's slender neck. He squeezed, slammed the side of her head off the window, and threatened her through clenched teeth.

"You lucky I ain't fucked you up for growing up around them niggas," he spat venomously, leaning in until his nose made contact with hers. He headbutted her, opening a laceration in her right eyebrow that instantly sent rivulets of blood sluicing down that side of her face. "I just lost my nephew because of the niggas you grew up with. My favorite fucking nephew. You better tell me something, and I mean something good, or you'll be waving hi to Skip before you know what hit you."

Tammy glowered at him for a long, silent moment, her small hands closed helplessly around his huge forearm, his thick, veiny hand gripping her throat and obstructing her windpipe. "You want me to tell you something?" Tammy asked rakishly. "I'll tell you something you really oughta know."

Steel loosened his hold on her throat, realizing only now that tears of rage had seeped out of his tear ducts, blurring his vision. He wiped them away with his free hand then used that same hand to slap Tammy across the face.

"You better tell me something," he repeated, speaking less aggressively this time. "Because if you don't..." He trailed off, leaving the threat hanging in the air.

"I'll tell you this." Tammy hawked up a good amount of snotty saliva and spit in Steele's big, ugly face. "You got about sixty seconds to live so make it count."

Steel's eyes widened with fear, and he raised his head to look out the window on Tammy's side of the SUV. Then, he turned to look out the front windshield then out the rear window, and finally, he twisted at the waist to peer back at his own window.

That was when he saw him. Markio Earl.

The bestselling novelist had another man standing next to him, a tall, brown skinned man with a green bandana tied around the lower half of his narrow face. Markio wore a red ski mask, but it was rolled up to his forehead, revealing his light brown face and the two dark teardrops inked below his left eye. A black Dodge Challenger Hellcat sat idling behind them, its driver and passenger doors open, its powerful engine growling like a pissed off lion.

Tammy took advantage of Steel's loose grip on her throat, yanking her door latch, shouldering the door open, and scrambling out from under him. She landed on her back just outside the door, and as she rose to her feet, she watched Markio and his partner in crime raise their mini-Draco pistols and take aim at Steel.

"See what all the internet dissing got you?" Markio asked coldly.

Markio pulled the ski mask down over his menacing face, and Tammy fled toward her parked Tahoe as the gunfire began.

Epilogue

"Well, well, well," said the woman who'd introduced herself to Markio as Teresa Dunlap. "Long time no see, huh?"

Markio chuckled and showed the undercover FBI agent a winning grin. "It ain't been but a few days," he said, pushing his laptop computer aside to gaze across the table at her. Three days had passed since Markio's fleeting war with Steel and the Black Gangster New Breeds. He hadn't left the Costilla Hotel since he and Slime had returned from gunning Steel down in the hospital parking lot. Now, he sat at a table inside El Padrino's — a five-star Mexican restaurant on the fifty-six floor of the massive skyscraper — putting the finishing touches on Chiraq Demons 4, his latest urban fiction novel. He studied the woman, whose real name was Deborah Wade, and wondered if she was really working on building a federal indictment against him.

She lowered her ample bottom onto the ladderback chair. She had a body like JT from the City Girls rap duo, and she had the lips to match. She had juicy, wet lips that were currently upturned in an appealing, seductive smile. She'd texted him this morning, asking if they could meet up for lunch, and he'd decided to take her up on the offer. He wanted to pick her brain to see if he could get her to reveal what all she knew about his gang.

"You're looking good this afternoon," she said, sweeping her gaze up and down his snow-white Louis Vuitton hoodie, sweatpants, and $100,000 Jordan X OVO sneakers. Clad in a curve hugging black bodysuit and knee high Balenciaga boots, she wasn't looking too shabby herself.

"Thank you." Markio wet his lips. He glanced from Debbie Wade to the words on the screen of his MacBook Pro and back to Debbie Wade again. "I'm single now, you know. Got to keep myself together for the next queen who comes my way."

"Yeah, I saw that on the Shade Room. Nikkia deleted all your pictures and unfollowed you. I've been a certified TSR Roommate from the start. If it's ever been posted on The Shade Room, I've seen it." She leaned forward and craned her neck to get a look at his computer screen. "What are you doing, writing another book?"

Markio nodded. "Might release this one next week. Been working on it off and on for the past few months."

"I don't know how you're able to come up with all these stories. They're so realistic, so clearly detailed. If it ever came out that some or most of your stories were actually true, I wouldn't be surprised."

Markio shrugged his shoulders dismissively and sat back in his chair, studying the FBI agent's posture, and her place mat, and the diverse crowd of men and women seated at the tables behind her. *How many of them are here for her?* Markio thought. She couldn't have come alone. Markio certainly hadn't. His two older cousins, Kay and Buck, were seated at the table to his left. He'd put up the two-million-dollar cash bond to free them from Cook County jail, and they'd walked out to two snow-white 2023 Rolls Royce Phantoms that set Markio back an additional $750,000. Kay's new girlfriend, JoJo, and Buck's wife, Lana, were seated with them. The four of them were eating their meals and chatting amongst themselves, none of them showing any sign that they'd arrived with Markio.

Two tables to Markio's right, Slime sat with Veronica C., the mother of his young daughter, Big Keanan, Markio's baby sister, Shakia, and Shakia's girlfriend, Shanese. At another table, Lil Luke and Jaybo sat with two more young gang members. Every man in Markio's entourage had a modified Glock pistol concealed somewhere on his waistline, and every woman had a modified, subcompact Glock pistol tucked in her Hermes Birkin bag.

"I don't live that lifestyle anymore," Markio said, shifting his gaze back to his computer screen. "All I do is write about that shit. Like Jay-Z said in that one song, 'It's only entertainment.' I write to entertain and educate the masses. To give 'em a glimpse into this Chicago gang culture. Ain't none of the shit true."

Debbie scoffed at the statement. "Yeah, right," she said, picking up a menu. "You are every bit as gangster as the characters in your books. Nobody could fake that. I've done my research on you. I mean, you are my favorite author. I have every book you've ever written."

She dug around in her black, leather Chanel shoulder bag. She rifled through if for a couple of seconds, retrieving an iPhone. She accessed her Kindle app and showed him that nearly every novel on her bookshelf was written by him.

Markio said nothing. He only stared at his book covers on the large screen of her smartphone and grinned. He had a lidded Styrofoam cup of Lean on the table in front of him. He removed the lid and took a small drink of the cold narcotic beverage. He wet his lips again.

"Don't look so nervous," Debbie said, beaming. "I'm not gonna rat you out or anything. I just find it intriguing that you're such a talented writer and a gangster at the same time. But anyways, when is *The Bird Man* movie coming? I heard my crush, Michael B. Jordan, is supposed to be starring in it."

"It's coming soon." Markio set his cup down and leaned forward, looking the federal agent in the eye. "I hope you know I did my research on you too."

Debbie's eyes flashed wide with alarm, but she recovered quickly. She brought herself time when a corpulent young waitress came over to take their order. Markio ordered chicken burritos, while Debbie opted for fully loaded beef and jalapeno nachos.

As the waitress walked away, Debbie said, "What do you mean you did your research on me? I've hardly even told you anything."

"You told me your name at Redbone's. Teresa Dunlap, right? I looked you up."

Markio showed a beaming smile when Debbie's troubled expression became more relaxed. Alexus had sent him links to the fake social media pages the FBI had created for Debbie under the name Teresa Dunlap as well as links to the real pages Debbie herself had created under the alias Angel Monroe to communicate with her family.

"You're from St. Louis," Markio said, adjusting his diamond flooded Rolex Sky Dweller wristwatch and taking another swig from his cup.

Debbie nodded. "The north side," she said. "I grew up in Riverview, lived on Scenic Drive all my life. My ex, Keyonte, used to sell dope out of the Drury Inn Hotel. He got set up by a nigga from Gibson Street Posse and ended up with a seventy-year sentence. I ain't had no good dick in my life ever since he left the streets, and that was six months ago."

It was Markio's turn to nod. His iPhone buzzed on the table. He picked it up and read the new text message and chuckled twice. "Life is crazy, ain't it?"

"What's that supposed to mean?" Debbie asked.

Markio shrugged. "Trick Daddy said that once, one of my favorite lyrics." He scooted back in his chair and got up. "I'll be right back. Gotta use the restroom."

Debbie gave him a warm smile and a subtle nod, and he walked off toward the restrooms. He saw that Slime was already entering the restroom ahead of him. Debbie's phone started ringing in her hand before Markio had even reached the restroom door, and when he looked back, she was on her feet, hurrying toward the elevators with a panic stricken look on her face.

Markio knew why she was in such a hurry to leave. The text message he'd received from Alexus read, "Ding dong, the witch is dead!" which meant that Enrique, the one handed Mexican sicario Alexus had put in charge of running the infamously ruthless Matamoros drug cartel, had ordered a sniper to go ahead with the plan to shoot Debbie Wade's mother, Barbara, in the head from a hundred yards away as the seventy-five year old woman sat on her front porch in Blue Springs, Missouri. Barbara's sister, Ruth, had been sitting beside the old lady, and Markio assumed it was Aunt Ruth who was on the line with Debbie now.

He entered the restroom with a triumphant smirk on his handsome, brown face and went straight to the sink to study his reflection in the mirror. He wore only one Cuban link necklace today, the thick one with the blinged out Millionaire Markio pendant hanging from it. Slime had gone into one of the toilet stalls. Markio turned away from the mirror and was about to say something to Slime when Slime began to speak with someone else, and it didn't take Markio but a couple of seconds to realize that Slime was on the phone.

"Hello? Kentrell?" There was a pause. Then, "Yeah, I'm in it, Slime. I ain't slid through there yet, but my people heavy in the street out here. Just getting my feet wet right now. Gon have my people take me out south so I can learn the lay of the land. Soon as I catch some'n, I'ma need that million dollars, ya heard me?"

Markio frowned. His head jerked back involuntarily. He turned back to the mirror to look himself in the eyes and ponder over what he'd just heard. Slime hadn't come to Chicago to get away from a Baton Rouge homicide investigation as he'd told Markio when they first spoke on the phone. No, Slime was here in Chicago for a different reason, to commit another homicide that Markio knew nothing about, apparently for a million-dollar payday.

Markio went to the urinal, squinting and nodding thoughtfully as the pieces came together in his brain. Slime often repeated a lot of things that Baton Rouge gangsta rapper NBA YoungBoy was fond of saying. NBA YoungBoy represented the north side of Baton Rouge and so did Slime. Slime had 38th tattooed on the back of his right hand and Chippewa St. inked on the back of his left one, Markio had no idea what block YoungBoy hailed from, but he'd heard several songs where the Louisiana rapper spoke of it being "North side thirty-eighth."

And the one thing Markio knew for certain was that NBA YoungBoy had an ongoing feud with Chicago drill rapper Lil Durk.

Up until now, Markio had been at peace. Alexus had forgiven his debt after learning of Voltaire's murder, but she'd had another shipment of drugs — five hundred kilos of cocaine for $14,000 a ki and a hundred kilos of fentanyl for $28,000 a ki — delivered to Markio's newest stash house in Maywood, Illinois, so again, he found himself owing millions of dollars to the Matamoras drug cartel ($9.8 million to be exact).

He'd blessed Tayja with twenty bricks of the white girl this time around. Fifty had gone to Buck, another fifty to Kay, and Markio's younger cousin, Bankroll Reese, had paid $4.4 million cash for two hundred of them. Small Body, a dope boy from Indianapolis' 40th and Boulevard set, had paid $2.2 million for a hundred of the cellophane wrapped cocaine bricks. Markio had fronted twenty bricks of soft to Tae and Dre, the King Squad twins from Harvey, Illinois for $27,500 a piece, and he'd paid Tayja to drop off an additional twenty bricks to one of Flocka's guys in Michigan City. The bricks to Flocka were free of charge, a payment for providing Voltaire's location to Markio three days ago. The last forty kilos of cocaine and the hundred bricks of fentanyl had gone to Bam for $4.88 million — $4 million for the pure fentanyl and $880,000 for the coke which Bam had also paid for in cash.

Tayja and the King Squad twins had paid Markio for their forty bricks the very next day, and he'd given Slime $1,000,000 of it for his supportive role in the killings of Voltaire, Skip, Hank, and Steel. Slime had used some of the money to lease a dark green Range Rover from Dub Life Autos and to rent out a nice, two-bedroom condo in the south loop for $4,200 a month.

Now thinking back to the Never Broke Again hoodie Slime had on when Markio first picked him up from the train station, Slime's gang affiliation seemed obvious. Markio just wished he would have noticed it earlier.

Shaking his head in frustration, he flushed the urinal, washed his hands, and left the restroom without saying a word to Slime. There was no sense in speaking on the puzzle he'd just pieced together. He figured he might need Slime's assistance in coming weeks. Markio had learned that Voltaire's Zoe Pound gang had trafficked his stolen drugs to Miami, and Markio was determined to recover that load. On top of that, word on the street was that a clique of Black Disciples from the low-end wanted Markio dead, and he wasn't going to let that slide either.

Markio Earl had sold off his entire six-hundred-kilogram load without ever touching a single gram, and now, he had over $30 million put away. He would deal with the Black Disciples first. Then the Haitians. And when it was all said and done, he'd get to the bottom of the situation with Kentrell — whoever that was.

Lock Down Publications and Ca$h Presents
Assisted Publishing Packages

BASIC PACKAGE	UPGRADED PACKAGE
$499	$800
Editing	Typing
Cover Design	Editing
Formatting	Cover Design
	Formatting
ADVANCE PACKAGE	**LDP SUPREME PACKAGE**
$1,200	$1,500
Typing	Typing
Editing	Editing
Cover Design	Cover Design
Formatting	Formatting
Copyright registration	Copyright registration
Proofreading	Proofreading
Upload book to Amazon	Set up Amazon account
	Upload book to Amazon
	Advertise on LDP, Amazon and
	Facebook Page

***Other services available upon request.
Additional charges may apply

Lock Down Publications
P.O. Box 944
Stockbridge, GA 30281-9998
Phone: 470 303-9761

Submission Guideline

Submit the first three chapters of your completed manuscript to ldpsubmissions@gmail.com. In the subject line add **Your Book's Title**. The manuscript must be in a Word Doc file and sent as an attachment. Document should be in Times New Roman, double spaced, and in size 12 font. Also, provide your synopsis and full contact information. If sending multiple submissions, they must each be in a separate email.

Have a story but no way to send it electronically? You can still submit to LDP/Ca$h Presents. Send in the first three chapters, written or typed, of your completed manuscript to:

LDP: Submissions Dept
P.O. Box 944
Stockbridge, GA 30281-9998

DO NOT send original manuscript. Must be a duplicate. Provide your synopsis and a cover letter containing your full contact information.

Thanks for considering LDP and Ca$h Presents.

NEW RELEASES

BLOODLINE OF A SAVAGE **BY PRINCE A. TAUHID**

THE MURDER QUEENS 4 **BY MICHAEL GALLON**

THE BUTTERFLY MAFIA **BY FUMIYA PAYNE**

KING KILLA 2 **BY VINCENT "VITTO" HOLLOWAY**

BABY, I'M WINTERTIME COLD 3 **BY MEESHA**

THESE VICIOUS STREETS **BY PRINCE A. TAUHID**

TIL DEATH 2 **BY ARYANNA**

CITY OF SMOKE 2 **BY MOLOTTI**

STEPPERS **BY KING RIO**

THE LANE **BY KEN-KEN SPENCE**

MONEY GAME 2 **BY SMOOVE DOLLA**

THE BLACK DIAMOND CARTEL **BY SAYNOMORE**

CRIME BOSS 2 **BY PLAYA RAY**

THUG OF SPADES **BY COREY ROBINSON**

LOVE IN THE TRENCHES 2 **BY COREY ROBINSON**

TIL DEATH 3 **BY ARYANNA**

THE BIRTH OF A GANGSTER 4 **BY DELMONT PLAYER**

PRODUCT OF THE STREETS **BY DEMOND "MONEY" ANDERSON**

Coming Soon from Lock Down Publications/Ca$h Presents

BLOOD OF A BOSS VI
SHADOWS OF THE GAME II
TRAP BASTARD II
By **Askari**

LOYAL TO THE GAME IV
By **T.J. & Jelissa**

TRUE SAVAGE VIII
MIDNIGHT CARTEL IV
DOPE BOY MAGIC IV
CITY OF KINGZ III
NIGHTMARE ON SILENT AVE II
THE PLUG OF LIL MEXICO II
CLASSIC CITY II
By **Chris Green**

BLAST FOR ME III
A SAVAGE DOPEBOY III
CUTTHROAT MAFIA III
DUFFLE BAG CARTEL VII
HEARTLESS GOON VI
By **Ghost**

A HUSTLER'S DECEIT III
KILL ZONE II
BAE BELONGS TO ME III
TIL DEATH II
By **Aryanna**

KING OF THE TRAP III
By **T.J. Edwards**

GORILLAZ IN THE BAY V
3X KRAZY III
STRAIGHT BEAST MODE III
By **De'Kari**

KINGPIN KILLAZ IV
STREET KINGS III
PAID IN BLOOD III
CARTEL KILLAZ IV
DOPE GODS III
By **Hood Rich**

SINS OF A HUSTLA II
By **ASAD**

YAYO V
BRED IN THE GAME 2
By **S. Allen**

THE STREETS WILL TALK II
By **Yolanda Moore**

SON OF A DOPE FIEND III
HEAVEN GOT A GHETTO III
SKI MASK MONEY III
By **Renta**

LOYALTY AIN'T PROMISED III
By **Keith Williams**

I'M NOTHING WITHOUT HIS LOVE II
SINS OF A THUG II
TO THE THUG I LOVED BEFORE II
IN A HUSTLER I TRUST II
By **Monet Dragun**

QUIET MONEY IV
EXTENDED CLIP III
THUG LIFE IV
By **Trai'Quan**

THE STREETS MADE ME IV
By **Larry D. Wright**

IF YOU CROSS ME ONCE III
ANGEL V
By **Anthony Fields**

THE STREETS WILL NEVER CLOSE IV
By **K'ajji**

HARD AND RUTHLESS III
KILLA KOUNTY IV
By **Khufu**

MONEY GAME III
By **Smoove Dolla**

MURDA WAS THE CASE III
Elijah R. Freeman

AN UNFORESEEN LOVE IV
BABY, I'M WINTERTIME COLD III
By **Meesha**

QUEEN OF THE ZOO III
By **Black Migo**

CONFESSIONS OF A JACKBOY III
By **Nicholas Lock**

JACK BOYS VS DOPE BOYS IV
A GANGSTA'S QUR'AN V
COKE GIRLZ II
COKE BOYS II
LIFE OF A SAVAGE V
CHI'RAQ GANGSTAS V
SOSA GANG III
BRONX SAVAGES II
BODYMORE KINGPINS II
By **Romell Tukes**

KING KILLA II
By **Vincent "Vitto" Holloway**

BETRAYAL OF A THUG III
By **Fre$h**

THE MURDER QUEENS III
By **Michael Gallon**

THE BIRTH OF A GANGSTER III
By **Delmont Player**

TREAL LOVE II
By **Le'Monica Jackson**

FOR THE LOVE OF BLOOD III
By **Jamel Mitchell**

SUPER GREMLIN 4 | KING RIO

RAN OFF ON DA PLUG II
By **Paper Boi Rari**

HOOD CONSIGLIERE III
By **Keese**

PRETTY GIRLS DO NASTY THINGS II
By **Nicole Goosby**

PROTÉGÉ OF A LEGEND III
LOVE IN THE TRENCHES II
By **Corey Robinson**

IT'S JUST ME AND YOU II
By **Ah'Million**

FOREVER GANGSTA III
By **Adrian Dulan**

GORILLAZ IN THE TRENCHES II
By **SayNoMore**

THE COCAINE PRINCESS VIII
By **King Rio**

CRIME BOSS II
By **Playa Ray**

LOYALTY IS EVERYTHING III
By **Molotti**

HERE TODAY GONE TOMORROW II
By **Fly Rock**

SUPER GREMLIN 4 | KING RIO

REAL G'S MOVE IN SILENCE II
By **Von Diesel**

GRIMEY WAYS IV
By **Ray Vinci**

Available Now

RESTRAINING ORDER I & II
By **CA$H & Coffee**

LOVE KNOWS NO BOUNDARIES I II & III
By **Coffee**

RAISED AS A GOON I, II, III & IV
BRED BY THE SLUMS I, II, III
BLAST FOR ME I & II
ROTTEN TO THE CORE I II III
A BRONX TALE I, II, III
DUFFLE BAG CARTEL I II III IV V VI
HEARTLESS GOON I II III IV V
A SAVAGE DOPEBOY I II
DRUG LORDS I II III
CUTTHROAT MAFIA I II
KING OF THE TRENCHES
By **Ghost**

LAY IT DOWN I & II
LAST OF A DYING BREED I II
BLOOD STAINS OF A SHOTTA I & II III
By **Jamaica**

LOYAL TO THE GAME I II III
LIFE OF SIN I, II III
By **TJ & Jelissa**

IF LOVING HIM IS WRONG…I & II
LOVE ME EVEN WHEN IT HURTS I II III
By **Jelissa**

SUPER GREMLIN 4 | KING RIO

BLOODY COMMAS I & II
SKI MASK CARTEL I, II & III
KING OF NEW YORK I II, III IV V
RISE TO POWER I II III
COKE KINGS I II III IV V
BORN HEARTLESS I II III IV
KING OF THE TRAP I II
By **T.J. Edwards**

WHEN THE STREETS CLAP BACK I & II III
THE HEART OF A SAVAGE I II III IV
MONEY MAFIA I II
LOYAL TO THE SOIL I II III
By **Jibril Williams**

A DISTINGUISHED THUG STOLE MY HEART I II &
III
LOVE SHOULDN'T HURT I II III IV
RENEGADE BOYS I II III IV
PAID IN KARMA I II III
SAVAGE STORMS I II III
AN UNFORESEEN LOVE I II III
BABY, I'M WINTERTIME COLD I II
By **Meesha**

A GANGSTER'S CODE I &, II III
A GANGSTER'S SYN I II III
THE SAVAGE LIFE I II III
CHAINED TO THE STREETS I II III
BLOOD ON THE MONEY I II III
A GANGSTA'S PAIN I II III
By **J-Blunt**

PUSH IT TO THE LIMIT
By **Bre' Hayes**

BLOOD OF A BOSS I, II, III, IV, V
SHADOWS OF THE GAME
TRAP BASTARD
By **Askari**

THE STREETS BLEED MURDER I, II & III
THE HEART OF A GANGSTA I II& III
By **Jerry Jackson**

CUM FOR ME I II III IV V VI VII VIII
An **LDP Erotica Collaboration**

BRIDE OF A HUSTLA I II & II
THE FETTI GIRLS I, II& III
CORRUPTED BY A GANGSTA I, II III, IV
BLINDED BY HIS LOVE
THE PRICE YOU PAY FOR LOVE I, II ,III
DOPE GIRL MAGIC I II III
By **Destiny Skai**

WHEN A GOOD GIRL GOES BAD
By **Adrienne**

A GANGSTER'S REVENGE I II III & IV
THE BOSS MAN'S DAUGHTERS I II III IV V
A SAVAGE LOVE I & II
BAE BELONGS TO ME I II
A HUSTLER'S DECEIT I, II, III
WHAT BAD BITCHES DO I, II, III
SOUL OF A MONSTER I II III
KILL ZONE
A DOPE BOY'S QUEEN I II III
TIL DEATH
By **Aryanna**

THE COST OF LOYALTY I II III
By Kweli

A KINGPIN'S AMBITION
A KINGPIN'S AMBITION **II**
I MURDER FOR THE DOUGH
By **Ambitious**

TRUE SAVAGE I II III IV V VI VII
DOPE BOY MAGIC I, II, III
MIDNIGHT CARTEL I II III
CITY OF KINGZ I II
NIGHTMARE ON SILENT AVE
THE PLUG OF LIL MEXICO II
CLASSIC CITY
By **Chris Green**

A DOPEBOY'S PRAYER
By **Eddie "Wolf" Lee**

THE KING CARTEL I, II & III
By **Frank Gresham**

THESE NIGGAS AIN'T LOYAL I, II & III
By **Nikki Tee**

GANGSTA SHYT I II &III
By **CATO**

THE ULTIMATE BETRAYAL
By **Phoenix**

BOSS'N UP I, II & III
By **Royal Nicole**

SUPER GREMLIN 4 | KING RIO

I LOVE YOU TO DEATH
By **Destiny J**

I RIDE FOR MY HITTA
I STILL RIDE FOR MY HITTA
By **Misty Holt**

LOVE & CHASIN' PAPER
By **Qay Crockett**

TO DIE IN VAIN
SINS OF A HUSTLA
By **ASAD**

BROOKLYN HUSTLAZ
By **Boogsy Morina**

BROOKLYN ON LOCK I & II
By **Sonovia**

GANGSTA CITY
By **Teddy Duke**

A DRUG KING AND HIS DIAMOND I & II III
A DOPEMAN'S RICHES
HER MAN, MINE'S TOO I, II
CASH MONEY HO'S
THE WIFEY I USED TO BE I II
PRETTY GIRLS DO NASTY THINGS
By Nicole Goosby

LIPSTICK KILLAH I, II, III
CRIME OF PASSION I II & III
FRIEND OR FOE I II III
By **Mimi**

TRAPHOUSE KING I II & III
KINGPIN KILLAZ I II III
STREET KINGS I II
PAID IN BLOOD I II
CARTEL KILLAZ I II III
DOPE GODS I II
By **Hood Rich**

STEADY MOBBN' I, II, III
THE STREETS STAINED MY SOUL I II III
By **Marcellus Allen**

WHO SHOT YA I, II, III
SON OF A DOPE FIEND I II
HEAVEN GOT A GHETTO I II
SKI MASK MONEY I II
By **Renta**

GORILLAZ IN THE BAY I II III IV
TEARS OF A GANGSTA I II
3X KRAZY I II
STRAIGHT BEAST MODE I II
By **DE'KARI**

TRIGGADALE I II III
MURDA WAS THE CASE I II
By **Elijah R. Freeman**

THE STREETS ARE CALLING
By **Duquie Wilson**

SLAUGHTER GANG I II III
RUTHLESS HEART I II III
By **Willie Slaughter**

SUPER GREMLIN 4 | KING RIO

GOD BLESS THE TRAPPERS I, II, III
THESE SCANDALOUS STREETS I, II, III
FEAR MY GANGSTA I, II, III IV, V
THESE STREETS DON'T LOVE NOBODY I, II
BURY ME A G I, II, III, IV, V
A GANGSTA'S EMPIRE I, II, III, IV
THE DOPEMAN'S BODYGAURD I II
THE REALEST KILLAZ I II III
THE LAST OF THE OGS I II III
By **Tranay Adams**

MARRIED TO A BOSS I II III
By **Destiny Skai & Chris Green**

KINGZ OF THE GAME I II III IV V VI VII
CRIME BOSS
By **Playa Ray**

FUK SHYT
By **Blakk Diamond**

DON'T F#CK WITH MY HEART I II
By **Linnea**

ADDICTED TO THE DRAMA I II III
IN THE ARM OF HIS BOSS II
By **Jamila**

YAYO I II III IV
A SHOOTER'S AMBITION I II
BRED IN THE GAME
By **S. Allen**

LOYALTY AIN'T PROMISED I II
By **Keith Williams**

TRAP GOD I II III
RICH $AVAGE I II III
MONEY IN THE GRAVE I II III
By **Martell Troublesome Bolden**

FOREVER GANGSTA I II
GLOCKS ON SATIN SHEETS I II
By **Adrian Dulan**

TOE TAGZ I II III IV
LEVELS TO THIS SHYT I II
IT'S JUST ME AND YOU
By **Ah'Million**

KINGPIN DREAMS I II III
RAN OFF ON DA PLUG
By **Paper Boi Rari**

CONFESSIONS OF A GANGSTA I II III IV
CONFESSIONS OF A JACKBOY I II
By **Nicholas Lock**

I'M NOTHING WITHOUT HIS LOVE
SINS OF A THUG
TO THE THUG I LOVED BEFORE
A GANGSTA SAVED XMAS
IN A HUSTLER I TRUST
By **Monet Dragun**

QUIET MONEY I II III
THUG LIFE I II III
EXTENDED CLIP I II
A GANGSTA'S PARADISE
By **Trai'Quan**

SUPER GREMLIN 4 | KING RIO

CAUGHT UP IN THE LIFE I II III
THE STREETS NEVER LET GO I II III
By **Robert Baptiste**

NEW TO THE GAME I II III
MONEY, MURDER & MEMORIES I II III
By **Malik D. Rice**

CREAM I II III
THE STREETS WILL TALK
By **Yolanda Moore**

LIFE OF A SAVAGE I II III IV
A GANGSTA'S QUR'AN I II III IV
MURDA SEASON I II III
GANGLAND CARTEL I II III
CHI'RAQ GANGSTAS I II III IV
KILLERS ON ELM STREET I II III
JACK BOYZ N DA BRONX I II III
A DOPEBOY'S DREAM I II III
JACK BOYS VS DOPE BOYS I II III
COKE GIRLZ
COKE BOYS
SOSA GANG I II
BRONX SAVAGES
BODYMORE KINGPINS
By **Romell Tukes**

THE STREETS MADE ME I II III
By **Larry D. Wright**

CONCRETE KILLA I II III
VICIOUS LOYALTY I II III
By **Kingpen**

THE ULTIMATE SACRIFICE I, II, III, IV, V, VI
KHADIFI
IF YOU CROSS ME ONCE I II
ANGEL I II III IV
IN THE BLINK OF AN EYE
By **Anthony Fields**

THE LIFE OF A HOOD STAR
By **Ca$h & Rashia Wilson**

THE STREETS WILL NEVER CLOSE I II III
By **K'ajji**

NIGHTMARES OF A HUSTLA I II III
By **King Dream**

HARD AND RUTHLESS I II
MOB TOWN 251
THE BILLIONAIRE BENTLEYS I II III
REAL G'S MOVE IN SILENCE
By **Von Diesel**

GHOST MOB
By **Stilloan Robinson**

MOB TIES I II III IV V VI
SOUL OF A HUSTLER, HEART OF A KILLER I II
GORILLAZ IN THE TRENCHES
By **SayNoMore**

BODYMORE MURDERLAND I II III
THE BIRTH OF A GANGSTER I II
By **Delmont Player**

SUPER GREMLIN 4 | KING RIO

FOR THE LOVE OF A BOSS
By **C. D. Blue**

KILLA KOUNTY I II III IV
By Khufu

MOBBED UP I II III IV
THE BRICK MAN I II III IV V
THE COCAINE PRINCESS I II III IV V VI VII
By **King Rio**

MONEY GAME I II
By **Smoove Dolla**

A GANGSTA'S KARMA I II III
By **FLAME**

KING OF THE TRENCHES I II III
By **GHOST & TRANAY ADAMS**

QUEEN OF THE ZOO I II
By **Black Migo**

GRIMEY WAYS I II III
By **Ray Vinci**

XMAS WITH AN ATL SHOOTER
By **Ca$h & Destiny Skai**

KING KILLA
By **Vincent "Vitto" Holloway**

BETRAYAL OF A THUG I II
By **Fre$h**

SUPER GREMLIN 4 | KING RIO

THE MURDER QUEENS I II
By **Michael Gallon**

TREAL LOVE
By **Le'Monica Jackson**

FOR THE LOVE OF BLOOD I II
By **Jamel Mitchell**

HOOD CONSIGLIERE I II
By **Keese**

PROTÉGÉ OF A LEGEND I II
LOVE IN THE TRENCHES
By **Corey Robinson**

BORN IN THE GRAVE I II III
By **Self Made Tay**

MOAN IN MY MOUTH
By **XTASY**

TORN BETWEEN A GANGSTER AND A
GENTLEMAN
By **J-BLUNT & Miss Kim**

LOYALTY IS EVERYTHING I II
By **Molotti**

HERE TODAY GONE TOMORROW
By **Fly Rock**

PILLOW PRINCESS
By **S. Hawkins**

SUPER GREMLIN 4 | KING RIO

SANCTIFIED AND HORNY
by **XTASY**

THE PLUG OF LIL MEXICO 2
by **CHRIS GREEN**

THE BLACK DIAMOND CARTEL
by **SAYNOMORE**

THE BIRTH OF A GANGSTER 3
by **DELMONT PLAYER**

BOOKS BY LDP'S CEO, CA$H

TRUST IN NO MAN
TRUST IN NO MAN 2
TRUST IN NO MAN 3
BONDED BY BLOOD
SHORTY GOT A THUG
THUGS CRY
THUGS CRY 2
THUGS CRY 3
TRUST NO BITCH
TRUST NO BITCH 2
TRUST NO BITCH 3
TIL MY CASKET DROPS
RESTRAINING ORDER
RESTRAINING ORDER 2
IN LOVE WITH A CONVICT
LIFE OF A HOOD STAR
XMAS WITH AN ATL SHOOTER

www.ingramcontent.com/pod-product-compliance
Lightning Source LLC
Chambersburg PA
CBHW071218260626
47162CB00004B/1339